Running the Gauntlet

Episode 4
of
The Missing Shield

Copyright:

First published in Great Britain, July 2018.

ISBN 978-1-912648-06-1

Cover design by The Chunky Designer, All Rights Reserved

Publisher L. L. Thomsen

Edited by Parkes Editing

Copyright © 2018 by L. L. Thomsen

All Rights Reserved.

The right of L. L Thomsen to be identified as the author of

this work has been asserted by her in accordance

with the Copyright, Designs and Patents Act 1988.

www.llthomsen.com

www.twitter.com/LLThomsen1

www.facebook.com/linda.thomsen.12979

www.facebook.com/themissingshield/

www.instagram.com/llthomsen

Contents

Acknowledgements:

To my husband for his patience and everlasting support that helped me realise my goals and dreams. Though not a geek and fantasy lover like myself, your trust and generosity means the world and this work would simply not have been possible without you.

To the brilliant, most inspiring, most important people of all: to the Owl and the Unicorn - my children; my muses - without whom my imagination would undoubtedly still be slumbering in a deep subterranean cavern. Even when dinner is a little late and I spend hours at the computer you still cheer me on - never lose the magic!

And last but not least: to the readers! Thank you for your interest, support and enthusiasm. Thank you for sticking with me and continuing on this journey - as a 100% indie author, you can never imagine how much this means to me. You make the story telling worthwhile!

Head's up From the Author:

Hi there and thank you for hopping onboard once more.

You will know by now that the lack of glossaries and maps is a deliberate choice on my part as I wanted you to enjoy the read without any distractions.

However, although the maps, glossaries, inventories, etc. are not printed here, it doesn't mean that they don't exist. I mean… this is epic fantasy after all!

So, as a self-respecting fantasy author I have of course elected to support the narrative with everything that will help you 'get your geek on' and I would therefore like to direct your attention to my official website www.llthomsen.com where you may explore titbits about the world of Dallancea at your own leisure, as well as look up names, terms, maps, information about the series - and much, much more.

The Story So Far

Solancei, Shield and childhood friend of Princess Iambre of Ostravah has gone missing after participating in an illegal fight in the westerly located city of Zanzier - the current location visited by Iambre and her staff on a celebration tour of the fifteen provinces. The princess' presence remains the dubious pleasure of her host, Lord Simarovien Zulavi, Knights Commander and 2nd Sword of Iambre's father, King Kaimar.

All Iambre knows is that Zulavi may or may not have a hand in Solancei's disappearance. Though scared and worried for her friend and cousin, she has been advised by her trusted Chief of Security, Eso Mehadja, that she must carry on diplomatic duties as though nothing is amiss, for a the revelation of the truth behind her Shield's disappearance could spell dire repercussions for herself and the Crown, and for Solancei.

Caught in a terrible place between worrying for her friend and allowing herself to finally forgive her love, Captain Metavo, for the truths spoken about the futility of their mutual affections, Iambre has furthermore reluctantly agreed to decommission the Captain once her party leaves Zanzier in less than ten days' time. As her mood deteriorates, it does not improve matters that Zanzier is a place of traditions and staid beliefs about duties and honour. Iambre is a trained diplomat, she puts on a good face and endures the droll atmosphere but even she has her limits - something that Lord Zulavi seems incapable of appreciating, as he continues to treat her with boorish snobbery and an insensitive attitude towards her station.

Meanwhile Solancei has landed in true trouble. Awakening in a dank dungeon she makes moves to escape Zulavi, but even her best efforts are soon thwarted, when - lost in the old tunnels below Zanzier - she encounters a nightmare creature known as a Demonai/Hyatt'Raah (Hyatt). Thought nothing more but figments of imagination and nursery rhymes, the discovery of these creatures puts the fear of death in her - the Hyatts somehow managing to penetrate her destabilising link with the State of Veranto to show her the horrendous truth of their bloodlust.

Fleeing in panic from what's in her head, she is caught once more by a now angered Lord Zulavi, who for all that he appears to want something from her, also seems keen to underscore that he will tolerate no more of her rebellious acts. She surrenders but is terrified upon realising that he seems intent on using her newly cultivated fear of the Hyatts against her - yet she can do nothing but comply as he forces her to return to the cavern where the Demonai are chained.

On his part, Zulavi is fascinated with the grey-eyed woman he's somehow landed himself. Originally set on executing her, first for the affront of breaking the law by duelling in a Jackal, and then for her bold escape attempts, he nevertheless finds that he cannot quite bring himself to follow through. The woman is a Master of Kizano and knows Veranto - the latter something he carries personal interest in.

Keen to either break her or entice her into sharing some of the secrets he is certain she contains, Zulavi both riles and cajoles her with stories of other female prisoners who've suffered death by his hand. However, the play takes an unplanned accidental push and a subsequent rescue from the fires of the lava pit that splits the cave, to finally get his prisoner to share her background story. Unconvinced of the truth, but still intrigued, Zulavi hopes that the arrival of another tiresome prisoner will serve a double purpose in tying up both a loose string and in further 'enticing' this woman who calls herself Cheska of New Wood to seeing sense and cooperate.

The Other Prisoner

Guest of honour? What flecking guest? What did he mean?

Solancei del'Isthalani Calverhana sent her unpredictable jailor a round-eyed look. Within her, the coldness stretched out, numbing her extremities. *Or was that the doings of the Veranto? Suddenly, she just couldn't tell.*

A stab of angst followed. *What if Simaro was bringing someone who knew her face? What if he was fetching someone who recognized her and knew her name?* From the tunnel corridor, the sounds of struggles grew steadily louder - curses and shouts of anger mingled with the clamour of metal and oaths, and soon, the discernible sounds of sporadic muffled punches too.

She glanced at Simaro again. He looked mildly expectant. From their ledge, in turn, the creatures growled, the vibration against her skin and bones raising a chilling anticipation in the air.

Solancei tried to steady her Link enough that she might drone out the fear they inspired - and not looking at them, she managed better than before, perhaps because her mind was undeniably pre-occupied.

"So what's this then?" she enquired with a mocking lilt to disguise the fluttering concern she knew might otherwise be creeping through, "Another blade-whore who did not know the appropriate difference between when to strike with the haitu and when to stroke your ego instead?"

Simaro huffed, seemingly bemused. "Of course not, grey-eyes - you were the first one to ever try that! No, as a matter of fact, I

1

pursued this one for a while before we caught him. Different story entirely!"

Solancei raised an eyebrow in query and swallowed a burst of morbid interest before it might sprout roots. For a moment she knew shame to feel such relief to have the attention diverted from herself - it was a cheap respite bought out of someone else's misery and it wouldn't last besides, yet-

Just keep your head and distance yourself! This has nothing to do with you; rise above it. Rise...

Solancei knew she lied to herself the moment the thought flashed through her mind. This had very much something to do with her, she knew it must have, and her gut twisted with renewed anxiety as she recalled that he'd wanted her to 'play witness'. *No... this could not be good at all.*

Her attention flickered to the soldiers. The guards they'd arrived with remained at the casual ready, their almost laid-back attitudes lending the scene a mundane aspect that she wouldn't have thought possible with the presence of the snarling Demonai in such close proximity. It sickened her. *It was all a little too much. Just a little too much!*

To gather her own wits, she shut her eyes in search of a moment to help smooth her mind but it seemed as tricky as fording the six-foot gap between the espaliered 'Aerie Promenade' and the squat armoury tower known simply as 'The Old Woman', back home.

It was a comparison that made her twitch within her skin. Castle Servangar sported thirteen towers: three of them so tall it felt like you could reach out and touch the harvest moon in summer but the two architectural features in question were without a doubt the hardest to navigate: you had to get into the narrow space in the first

2

place, then you had to swing and let go with one hand, simultaneously grasp for the water sprout on the far side as you moved - and it could be done, certainly, but it required you to use the momentum just right; it required that you committed and let go to twist, so that for one split heartbeat, you simply soared without a handhold above the empty space of the narrow shaft. *It was stupid - there was a perfectly serviceable staircase all the way to the Aerie Promenade and the gossip one got to overhear when taking the 'hard' way not even worth the light of day, except-*

Well, except for just that once.

Her heart contracted almost painfully at the memory and she grimaced softly. She didn't want to think of that time, but it was evidently a good distraction. In all her years at Servangar, she'd made the 'jump' over that narrow shaft precisely five times: the fourth time still for thrills, never dreaming she'd overhear the confessions of betrayal from the very lips of a person she'd come to trust as a friend, and the fifth time...

Well... suffice it to say that it was a difficult climb and that for varying reasons both final trials had sucked the energy right out of her, but perhaps that was why she'd recalled those queer events because it had been just like now! *She felt drained beyond care...*

She clenched her teeth, finding in spite all, a little anger still within. *Gods! Why couldn't she seem to find the stillness of mind? If she were to ruin the Link with useless thoughts of the past, then-*

Feeling crippled she opened her eyes - just in time to visually greet two additional guards and their unwilling charge emerging from the tunnel. The new guards wore expressions of barely-contained nuisance, unsuccessfully hidden beneath stone-faced masks of familiarity and she could read their mounting displeasure

3

as they half-dragged, half-beat a bedraggled, shackled prisoner into view.

A sight to melt her own concerns, her spirit immediately cringed with sympathy. Against the two soldier's stout arming-doublets and padded breeches, the prisoner's attire looked beggared. What he wore was an assembly of ragged, perhaps once well-made, garments - consisting of a billowing, torn shirt that might originally have been white but now suffered an ugly array of grime and stains, whilst his legs were covered by a baggy pair of breeches of such an indeterminate material that she guessed at cotton, not leather, only due to the tear across one knee. Underneath him, the prisoner's feet were bare, tawny and scruffy; he was void of adornment or heraldry - yet the sight of him still touched her as much as the treatment he received. *How long had this man been at Simaro's mercy? Weeks? Months?*

Attempting to catch a glimpse of his features, Solancei ran her eyes repeatedly over the un-kept tangle of dark revels that hung off his skull to disguise most of the long salt-and-pepper whiskers covering the down-cast face like the badge of a war veteran, but she failed to note anything of distinguishing concern.

Unease clawing within, melting the imaginary ice just enough to help her pull closer the Link instead, she stared down on her own hands, anxious with new questions. *Was this to be her future too? Was she to be locked up, shackled and beaten and dragged forth on display at his whim? Was this what her jailor would subject her to if she did not accommodate him?*

She shivered and looked at Simaro in his brocade and silk. He was distracted. *Mayhap she ought to steal his dagger now and slice her own throat? Mayhap she would not get another chance?*

4

She gazed upon the shaggy prisoner's head of wild hair, feeling trapped. The man was an ugly display of her captor's lack of mercy: a powerful statement - and as she watched in mounting horror, her mind shied away from the possibility that she could be him, even as the prisoner angrily yanked at his chains, receiving no quarter for the effort as he was dragged forth.

No matter the offence, this was not fair - but was this Simaro's intention? That she should witness his utter power over a fellow prisoner so that she might feel inspired to comply?

Solancei opened her mouth to speak, then closed it again. *She could not stop them. Whatever she said would not be enough.* She had no authority here. Sure, Simaro might not kill her for the presumption, but... but her loyalty was to Iambre, not some foreign prisoner. *Whatever urges or feelings of sympathy she might be experiencing, she must rise about it. She must!*

Shackles rattled as the prisoner was flung forward, grunting as he landed in a heap at Simaro's feet and Solancei clenched her teeth, swallowing a bout of righteous new anger. For long moments the prisoner lay still, panting hard as though he'd just collapsed after a long run and couldn't possibly move another inch, but there was something about the way he clenched his dirty fingers into fists so hard the scraped knuckles stood out white; something in the way he let his too-long, un-kept ravels of hair shadow his lowered head and eyes...

And then she realised what. *Simaro's prisoner wasn't so much trying to recover as he was trying to gather his faculties before facing the man whose feet he was close enough to kiss. Maybe he was seething at his own inability to influence the situation; maybe...*

Across the chasm, the Demonai roared, their sound one of frustration it seemed.

Both Solancei and the prisoner trembled simultaneously. *Just as she thought herself in control, they reminded her vividly that she was not! Those aberrations seemed like shadows, clinging to her mind: ever present, ever on the cusp of sending her running! Did the prisoner feel the same?*

Solancei noted another shudder pass through the unfortunate man, the reaction vivid enough to transfer through the rags of his formerly-handsome shirt; it surprised her to realise that where one of the wide sleeves had been torn, the skin beneath looked swarthy - like that of an Imkarahian...

She licked blistering lips, thinking hard. Other than Bilandro Metavo, she knew no Imkarahians on sight; as she was aware, only a handful could be found at Court, but she could be wrong of course. *Indeed, maybe this man was just swarthy due to the grime that covered him.*

The prisoner shuddered again, the ripple of his discomfort travelling the length of his wiry frame, almost as if the man could not help himself. He was still breathing fast - unnaturally so, she thought. *Was he sick?*

Solancei threw Simaro a quick look, concern and resentment mingling - yet those hard facial planes were unreadable, as he gave the prisoner by his feet an emotionless stare.

Perhaps feeling her scrutiny though, Simaro looked up. For a moment his expression remained bland as he held her stare, then a wrinkle of unspent emotion passed across his face, gone before she could interpret it, and he grunted, looking back at the prisoner. "Lord Angemar. Well met."

6

Simaro's flippant tone seemed at odds with the sudden tightness she spied in the set of his shoulders and she watched the prisoner for a sign that might create a sliver of understanding, wondering what the story was. As it were, the man did not respond, but she saw him clench his fists even tighter for just a heartbeat and from that alone it was clear that he'd heard Simaro just fine.

As if understanding this too, Simaro sighed, shifting the weight from one foot to the other as he crossed his arms. "Oh fine, I see that we have caught you at a bad time, Cillario. Pity I suppose. A little less interaction might have been preferable but I regret that our appointment cannot wait. You see... I have this other visitor. Would that you could help, dear Angemar."

The prisoner seemed to still at the sound of his name: as though someone had lowered a sword point to his neck, but then he shuddered, the breath whistling in his chest and he seemed to collapse a little as his frame was suddenly beset by a new series of tremors.

It was hot in the cavern. Was he fevered - or were the shakes perhaps an effect of the Demonai? Solancei looked from the prisoner to Simaro and back. Staring at both men, she had a really odd feeling that she was posed on some horrible junction where no matter which trajectory presented her, the only routes to follow, would be either 'bad' or 'horrendous'. *Angemar? Was that even a name she'd ever heard?*

Solancei caught her bottom lip between her teeth, warring...

It was a cowardly thing to be thankful for, but at least it did not seem familiar. Angemar? She twirled the name in her mind, but her memory seemed clear. *Angemar? Angemar Cillario?* She guessed it could be Imkarahian, but on second thought he did not look Imkarahian after all - not when you knew what to look for...

Solancei stared at the prisoner's silver-flecked crown of dark hair, wishing she'd caught a better look of his face.

"Come, come now Angemar," Simaro coaxed like he was talking to an old friend caught sulking. "Angemar, gather your wits. You're making my guest frown. The two of you have much in common. I need you to speak sense to her now."

The man on the ground issued a half-snort, half-laugh, an oddly laconic sound that seemed to mock both himself as well as Simaro.

"Oh, but this is precious," the prisoner spat with gravelly contempt directed at the rock between his hands, "The last time-"

The rest of Angemar's words died in his throat as a tremor interrupted to rake the length of his frame, robbing him of intensity.

Rolling his eyes with a hint of theatrical flair, Simaro drew a deep breath. "Very well, I will admit I was not particularly diplomatic in my choice of words, but-"

"Pah!" the prisoner snorted though nor quite recovered, his fists digging into the floor as he shifted to push himself up just high enough to lift his head and chest. "If... if I recall this right, the last time you saw me, you told me that you had no further need of me and that I should stop ranting or you'd take my tongue. Then you left me to rot in the dark!"

The prisoner paused and snorted as if amused, but his tone was turning acerbic, "With all the things you've done, you rancid piece of Venzoian whore's spawn, what in Alérathnar's name could it be that now compels you into thinking that I will care one fleck what you want?!"

8

For a moment Angemar stared through the fall of matted hair directly at Simaro, his detrimental defiance pouring forth like a challenge through the gleam of his dark eyes as well as in the intensity of his pose. Solancei used the moment to take a hard look at the man, but...

In spite of her fears, she felt almost morbidly disappointed. She did not know him, but who was he then?

She looked back to Simaro who now pursed his lips and shook his head. "Angemar, Angemar, Angemar... do you really wish to go there? Can you at least not make an eloquent attempt? Your head seems in the right place today, so do this now - if not for me, then for my guest?"

Solancei saw the prisoner's eyes narrow and he quivered. "Your head seems also in the right place today," he retorted, "Go quiff a goat!"

"Oh, this is pointless!" Simaro growled, flinging his head back with an impatient gesture to stare at the shadows. A hard sigh, then he flicked his chin towards his men, "Get him off the floor now and let's get things moving. The hour is drawing late and this hole is roasting; I grow weary and in need of a drink."

"Then go spit in the eyes of the Mad Ones!" Angemar coughed at him in a voice that cracked from anger and misuse as he raised it to be heard over the scramble of feet and chains when the guards caught a hold of him. "I'm sure they'll gladly pull out their pricks and piss down your gullet in response! In truth, if you beg her right, Kira'Cha might even squat over-"

The prisoner coughed and was cut short as the guards yanked him upright, the horse-faced one on the left throwing him a punch to the lower ribs either out of sheer meanness or else to silence his

9

insults. Solancei cringed in sympathy as the fist connected, hearing quite clearly how the prisoner gulped in pain as he was robbed of breath and doubled over.

She frowned with ill-hidden aggravation, her resentment growing icy. Simaro had stepped back - but said nothing when horse-face's fist connected with the prisoner again, never giving him a chance to straighten. *It was not fair! Regardless of the crimes committed, how could Simaro let them beat a sick, shackled man?*

"Sure, sure, sure... 'entice' me if you would, with a beating-" Angemar coughed, then coughed again as he began to laugh, "-it has worked in the past, of course; maybe it will again!"

The ill-kept man coughed again, his mocking tone absolving into a growl of anger as a new involuntary shiver passed through his body. The guard responded by landing him another punch and Angemar's legs buckled so that he would have sagged to his knees all over, were it not for the guards' support.

"I have nothing more to say," he gasped at the floor, a few soft tremors rushing through his frame, "We were done you stinking sack of offal! And we will stay done!"

Solancei watched Simaro's mouth twist - that same expression that spoke of a bad mouthful of wine swallowed - and a sudden realisation hit her. *The prisoner did not sound Imkarahian at all - in fact, he spoke with no accent, almost as if he'd never acquired one - however, he did sound learned. With a hint of courtly dignity as well: like a Senator or a Scholar, even.*

Her attention crossed to the soldiers, then back at Simaro as he flicked them a tiny negative gesture with the fingers of his left hand, thus halting their action before the next blow could fall. *What was Simaro thinking?* A pensive frown was already exchanging places

10

with the expression of displeasure and Solancei looked at the prisoner as he hung between the two guards, bent over and quivering from soft tremors.

There was a part of her that mentally saluted this Angemar and his seemingly unyielding character and baleful insults, but at the same time, there was also something profoundly upsetting about it: as though she was watching this happen to an old friend and not a total stranger. *Which meant that she was somehow getting too absorbed in the spectacle after all! But was it any wonder?* This had not a sliver of the supposed Zanzierian Chivalry about it and yet she'd come to expect as much from Simaro, which - because of his strange notions of right and wrong - was beginning to form its own mangled pattern of predictability. She wondered why Angemar was daring Simaro thus? Indeed, what he could possibly hope to achieve other than another beating?

Without intending to, she sidled closer to Simaro.

"Is he sick?" she enquired, somehow feeling the need to whisper like she might have done had she been standing in an infirmary next to somebody's sickbed.

Simaro's forehead creased. "Why do you ask, grey-eyes? What would it differ?"

Solancei shrugged, then had to cut back on the sarcasm as she quietly noted, "He seems unwell, that's all. Maybe a bit of sunshine…?"

Simaro's huff sounded close to a guffaw. "And what are you now, Cheska grey-eyes from New Wood? A Wise Woman?"

Solancei bit her lip, clasping her arms tightly across the chest. "You name me tricky, but you are the one who plays games. I told you already that I do not like games! Why is he here? What are your intentions? You spoke of us reaching understanding and of finishing something? How is that man relevant?"

"My Gods, dear girl, are you really that clueless?" Simaro met her eyes. "Do you not see? I wish for him to tell you how he went wrong so that you might learn from his mistakes, but-"

Without a sound of warning, the prisoner chose that very blink to attack. Solancei did not even have time to gape or know shock, it happened so suddenly. From the corner of her eye, there was a flash of movement as Angemar shifted, somehow turning and wrenching himself free of horse-face's hands, simultaneously swinging a fist for the guard to the other side.

It hit the target like a hammer blow.

Reacting, horse-face growled, reaching for his short-sword, but he got no further than touching the hilt before the prisoner shifted like a true Kizano Master - shackles no hindrance - to lay an open-handed punch directly into the soft flesh of the guard's throat.

In response, horse-face made a strange choking sound, retching and clutching his neck as he fell back.

Still, Angemar did not stop. As if he'd been possessed with the speed and strength of Anchan'Chi Himself, he swooped forward in a blink within blinks, his focus solely honed on Simaro, and Solancei had a beat to see the hated man's winter-cold eyes widen in alarm - then things became a blur, everything happening at once.

A quick-witted soldier in Zanzier colours tried to swoop in and grapple Angemar, but the prisoner did not even miss a step as he threw the man off with one abrupt swipe of his elbow that saw the soldier fall back, comically colliding with two colleagues as they came forth. One righted himself and managed not to go down in a tangle of limbs and blades but Angemar simply laughed as he

12

kicked out, flawlessly executing the form of *crescent-moon-ascending.*

His timing was perfect - *Solancei could have envied him the finesse under such circumstances* - but the way the man swivelled his attention back to Simaro like a murderous viper startled from its den, had her gasping with surprise instead. *The prisoner was sleek and fast like a White Assassin; he seemed possessed...*

...possessed with madness!

Without warning, her world tilted, scattering her thoughts, as Simaro gripped her arm and spun her out of the way with a flurry of movement and a harsh yell for the attention of the two nearest soldiers to catch her.

It was all he had time to do. Angemar fell on him like a starved hunting cat, bearing them both to the ground: he atop Simaro. Solancei didn't bother to hide her grin and tried in vain to twist her neck to keep the combatants in view but she lost sight of them as the soldiers caught a hold of her.

For a blink, all she heard was a series of punches connecting with flesh, along with sounds of angry men trying to intercept. Gulps of pain followed - but who'd hit who?

She clawed at the soldiers, fighting to get herself spun back around again and finally managed to right herself enough to swing her eyes back to the squabble.

What she witnessed made her crack another smile. Angemar was landing two successive blows to Simaro's face, the angry force behind each succinct hit delightfully evident as Simaro reeled on the defence.

It made the man to her left cuss in horror and she could almost feel the indecision rolling off the two guardsmen then. Of course, their first instinct would be to fly to their Lord's aid - but other soldiers were already moving, springing back from whatever punishing acts Angemar had treated them to and they'd be upon the two fighters in a flicker of an eye.

Her two guards saw the inevitable too; she felt them steady - and then it was suddenly all over. Angemar made an attempt to evade but two soldiers tackled him in tandem, pulling him off Simaro with brute force, helped now by another who slid between the mad prisoner and their unfortunate master, raising a wicked-looking long dagger to staunch the man's irate struggles. It brought Angemar back into himself a little, but for a beat, it looked to Solancei as though he was ready to fall on the Zanzierian blade and she clearly heard both her guards hiss sharply in dismay.

"Don't kill him!" Simaro yelled, staggering to his feet, his finery in disarray, his sword and dagger tangled. The soldier complied, shifting his blade sharply while the others wrenched Angemar backwards till he was pressed against a jagged outcrop.

The scene raised goose bumps along Solancei's arms, and all the while the Demonai never quietened. Their growls were low - of that same vibrating cadence as before - and it seemed to get right beneath her skin.

She refused to look their way, however, and this time her resistance seemed to bolster her nerves. Her guards had been prudent enough to shift them back towards the tunnel entrance to avoid getting tangled with the fighters and for a blink, her heart seemed to beat faster as she considered her luck. *All the remaining men were distracted by Angemar and Simaro... if ever there were a better chance...*

14

The guard on her left was a short solid man with a furrowed forehead and a tidy, sandy-coloured moustache. From the brief glimpses she'd had of him and the fellow on the right, they both looked to be veterans, but not of the elite type. *Dare she try?*

Her eyes went to Angemar where they'd pinned him against the rock. If she got his attention, he might win free again - the man had talent in spite of ill health; they might help each other; it could work – however if she fought again and lost; if she went up against Simaro again and did not secure the upper hand...? *Well, he'd surely gut her as promised!*

For a beat, her desire warred with fear and her guilt seemed to deepen then. *She must think of Iambre. Angemar was but a stranger, whereas Iambre...*

The world above seemed suddenly little more than a dream; a fantasy of smoke and mirrors. *The light-headed feeling she'd previously known came back.* Shame that Iambre would never know how it cost her to acknowledge the need for care today; shame Iambre would never know how Solancei's newfound restraint had won out in favour over her usual intransigent seed of rebellion, but for Iambre-

"You treasonous, rancid turd!" she heard Angemar snarl, as another man - *horse-face?* - dealt him a resounding slap for some offence she'd failed to pay attention. "You will all die with the sounds of your own whimpering screams for company! You will not-"

Angemar launched himself forward, surprising everyone, but unlike before he never truly managed to threaten Simaro with physical contact as he was pulled back under control by his now-vigilant guards.

15

Growling under his breath the man rested back, panting with exertion, and Solancei bore witness with pent-up breath as Simaro stepped closer then, his face shrouded by feral anger as he proceeded to wipe away the blood still trailing from his nose. *She almost couldn't mask a sick smile for the fortune, but-*

Instead of a smile, a soft groan escaped her and she felt ill. Something gnawed at her spirit; a strange feeling of wrongness that seemed to be developing irrespective of the Veranto. She thought she'd been aware but had managed to suppress the feeling, yet now it intensified and all at once her core fell cold: like a rushed flare of *ice fang* - a twist of nature that she hadn't witnessed since childhood.

Instead of frosting the dark walls of Ivanor in a few split breaths of fear, though - the sensation flowed like travelling liquid within her bones. Something seemed to split within her suddenly - as if another part of her was inexplicably ready to claw its way out in order to assure self-preservation, and then-

She gasped, too stomped to fear, but half-expecting a gust of icy breath to leave her mouth on the exhale. It didn't, yet she was forced to swallow hard, the coldness still rising and now so harsh that the feeling finally scared her because amidst the uncanny invading sensation, the State of Veranto was slipping, melting, and slowly shifting...

Desperation expanded like claws within her: for a moment heightening everything. Simaro was watching Angemar as if he was looking at a worm to be squashed beneath the heel of his boot and Solancei knew in that blink that she'd probably never see Iambre again.

NO!

16

Sheer need - or sheer luck - she'd never know which, but the ice retreated a sliver then and in the non-existing space that flexes between past and future, the State of Veranto rose up like a wall within her, dulling the frozen heat and neutralizing...

Calm proceeded to fill her. *The right kind.* Her mind settled... *wherewithal returned...*

The prisoner had a bloody nose and a new hollow scrape along one cheek and she understood by the scene that Simaro had paid him back in kind. It was an unnerving thing to realise that for a moment she'd been lost within herself beyond the normal world, but then even that didn't seem to matter. *For the first time the prisoner's dark gaze centred squarely on her face - and as she met his deep-set eyes, now also for the first time - a peculiar sentiment seemed to jostle the stranger's features.*

Eyes flaring wide, she heard the moment his breath caught then released as though he'd been punched, followed by a strangled sound, and Solancei recoiled, understanding rising the fine hairs on her nape. *For a blink it meant nothing, then new fear snapped through her, drenching, and jolting her connection with Veranto. How...?*

With an intake of air, she calmed herself through the Link, so impossibly pleased that it complied, because....

Because this Angemar knew her! She did not know him, so how could he possibly know her - but he did! Bloody fleck, evidently he did!

With a Weave

Gasping like a messenger out of breath and struggling frantically to stay within the present, young Far Seer Nefer'Kemnebit, barely managed to keep her composure as belated fear lashed into her.

Clasping the hand of her new mentor with a strength that she hadn't known she possessed, she felt a new base desperation to hold on - and just then he was the only solid person in a world of uncertainty. *Anchoring herself onto him was her only choice!*

But her new tutor, Sinu, seemed to understand. The vial of herbal essence that he held under her nose never wavered as he managed to prop her upright so that she might feel more comfortable; in his eyes, she saw a new light: an edge of something she'd not seen moments ago. *An edge of speculation.*

Feeling her faculties return, Nefer'Kemnebit experienced a rush of self-conscious chagrin. She had never lost herself so totally to a vision without the crystals before - and on top of what had happened earlier, it was frightening. Without really knowing how, her visions had claimed her - and for the second time in a day no less - only now she'd spun so completely out of control that she couldn't even decipher why anymore.

Her head churned with the implications and after-shock though. *Dear spirits, what would have happened if Sinuhé had not been present to bring her out of the vision when he did? Her Sire would've had to step in and the scandal-!*

She wouldn't even wish to think about it - but for a moment it had seemed as though breath had failed, not only the Twin, but also her! *She could feel the desperate sensation; the sense of obliterating confusion that there was nothing but blood, and the pressure within of-*

Scared by her pseudo-memories, she shook herself. Back from the cusp of oblivion, she marvelled that her tutor had never flinched from the grip she had on his poor hand and she was grateful when she heard his whispers of unknown words and felt them work their calming influence. Slowly, their gentle demand steadied her until she felt herself centred wholly back in the present; the tingle of healing magic, though not unexpected, had stolen past her Benedictions like a soft touch of a dove's feather, not burrowing deeper now, but retreating...

"My Lady Sheriti: well done! Do not let the possible events control you! First rule: you always control them! Well done!"

Sinu's voice seemed distant but she stayed with him, conquering the need to preserve an imaginary portal to retain a link with the rapidly receding images. She felt drained. *There was nothing to be proud of! How could he praise her? She had controlled nothing!*

Feelings of a different kind building, an acute irrational sense of loss filled her as though inspired by magic. *She must go to the Council. If her new tutor drew on Weaves this close to the Watchéran without consequence, then maybe-*

"Sinuhé, Esteemed Tutor, I beg of you: hear me." The formal words came rushed; without reserve now and seemed somehow too insignificant to precede what she was about to tell him but she ignored the feeling. Swallowing to relieve the sudden knot in her throat she blinked to clear rising tears from her eyes, recalling now that she'd best remain carefully correct, so as to assure herself of Sinuhé's undivided attention.

With the desired effect in mind, she said, "I have seen the promise of a terrible misfortune. I see it over and over, but always different, always never as the time before, but it is Truth! The lady of Fjeer'dhanlaar loses her twin sister and also her love for the Mshai! Sinuhé, esteemed tutor, I do not presume to order you as only He-Who-Is can do, but we have to stop it; somehow we must see them right because this is not how it's supposed to be. The ones I see; they are not of this world and I fear that my vision heralds the beginning of the True End if we do not intervene. Both twins must live! The Mshai must live! Otherwise, we are set on course to drown the Golden Eye forever in the ashes that will fall! Esteemed Master, it is not just we of the Sabén-Heshep who are at risk, but everyone across the Glorious Lands. Everyone!"

Nefer'Kemnebit drank a large mouthful of the cool wine from the cup her tutor had thrust into her hands, the quality of the liquid barely a distraction even if the strong flavour threw her.

"My dear one, those are serious words." Sinuhé's deep eyes bore into hers, projecting mild weariness for her warning, yet he did not laugh at her claims, nor did he try to dismiss urgency below a fall of arguments.

"Esteemed Tutor, I am most pressingly aware." Releasing his hand to steady herself and the goblet of cool, tart wine, Nefer cast down her eyes.

Something obsidian lay at her feet, in spite all, hooking her attention. *Sweet Maker, the panther!*

As though it had sought shelter, the little black ornament rested on the floor in the shadows between her feet where she must have dropped it whilst semi-comatose and somehow heartened by the sight, she scooped it up. Clasping it hard for comfort, the sharp ears

20

bit into her palm, but she didn't care - it was Reality, and in a flash, she realised its possible purpose.

"Hmmm, yes... yes, I believe you are very aware, Dear Heart." As if he'd read her mind, Sinuhé raised a knowing eyebrow.

Replacing the cap on the small vial of Morning Glory with a show of deft absent-minded routine, the older man pocked the drops in a double fold of his pleated toga and appraised her with a serious mien that made her clasp the cat tighter.

"I would beg of our Mshai not to pay any mind to these black-outs of hers," her Sire implored of Sinuhé, drawing the attention of them both.

With what Nefer would only describe as a mystical light in his eyes, her Sire continued, "She... this is what she is occasionally like. This is why I hope you might help. Her talk of the Twins and a blue-haired Mshai's, of death and of love - whilst they upset my subjects and drill inspiration for fey speculations of doom - surely you would concur with the Chief of Vectors that those dreams of hers are but fabrications to suit a young mind? Even Weaver Ti'Anakit'Suh has determined Nefer'Kemnebit's peculiar extra 'visions' must be amalgamations, but with this new frequency..."

As the Sabén-Heshep exulted Watchéran felt silent, Sinuhé looked strangely uncertain, but then he offered her father a serene nod. "Yes... yes, of course, I can see that this must seem stressing. Still, I have observed similar cases in the past. With temperance and guidance, the young ones usually outgrow their quirks. What is presently happening will not be detrimental to her later Affinity. All will be well. I will guide her through this."

Nefer wanted to protest but her voice seemed to lock and so she kept silent. Something in Mshai Sinuhé's tone made her feel as

21

though she was watching an illusion of sorts, but she couldn't feel the pollution of any Weaves in the air, not even the tiniest disturbance to explain her odd sentiment. It unsettled her. Like finding a book out of place or a new crack in a paving stone - both things were terribly mundane but she didn't like to discover that they happened. It played hopscotch with her perceived order of events and it always triggered these less than desirable reactions to certain aspects of her Affinity. Now her Sire looked ill at ease too - something she had never been permitted to witness before - and indeed for all she knew, this could very well be the first time He felt such a way!

It was yet another break in normality and like the wrath of an Elemental, it made new shimmering pictures form and undulate, dwindle and re-form in her mind: *pulling, whispering...*

Clutching the small black figurine hard, the images receded though - and trying her hardest to recall the strident scent of the Morning Glory over that of swords and blood and sorrow, she managed to ride above the flow that tugged for attention.

It staggered, but the achievement thrilled her. *It might not last, but it was the best she'd thus far ever managed!.*

"Her Sire's voice cut in, "You see, the importance she places upon these visions and the need to avert them...?"

As her father's voice petered out, his odd uncertainty clearly transferring, Nefer stared at her drink, the icy condensation long gone to leave behind only a clammy film of dew.

Unease returning, she took a sip anyway. *There was a physical pressure in the air suddenly, not from Sinuhé, but from-*

A sudden glow of power riding off her Sire like a waterfall bleeding out of him made Nefer want to shrink to the size of an ant as His

22

eyes went momentarily golden. To her mental and physical sight it made the day seem uncomfortably dazzling, the searing brightness of multiple suns too hard to withstand by natural means, but then it stopped, the sky instantly dulling in the aftermath and the air temperature dropping for a blink to re-decorate her beaker with velvety frost before recalibrating to normal.

To the sweep of a rushing new breeze picking up and setting alive the red awning and the servants' flowing costumes of thin pale cotton, the Watchéran said, "Well... my confidence in you was never ill-placed, Guardian, that I cannot dispute - but you see how my lands fare; how I fare. Perhaps 'disturbing' is not the word I should have chosen; perhaps-"

Her Sire halted, the muscles under his tight black skin shifting as he sighed, then said, "Guardian Chronicler, the Maker help us: she may not be speaking of *the Twins,* but the sooner we can alleviate the fears brought to life by speculations and rumours, the better for everyone! The Tapestry weaves a clear path of the future. There's been nothing to indicate otherwise; nothing. Yet for certain fickle individuals to believe it might be so just because Our Best-Loved Daughter speaks the words...?!

"Well in any case, those of us of the higher Tiers have remained certain that her dreams are nothing to be concerned with. I... I only hope your guidance will help her focus to conquer and shed this... this curious 'defect'. This is what matters, Guardian. This - and the rest will assuredly follow! "

"Oh I am confident we might be able to sort out the confusion surrounding this," Sinuhé allowed with a tiny frown - and for a wonder, Nefer was inexplicably convinced that he did not side with her father or the Chief of Vectors in this. She couldn't pinpoint the origin of her sudden insight, though - like that fey sensation experienced moments earlier, there was nothing to suggest the flow of magical manipulation because yet again she felt not a thing out of place. *Still... suddenly she found herself considering the possibility that Sinuhé Sedjem-Alhath'naar might just take her side where all the others... where all the others, did not.*

Control returned to him, the Watchéran seemed yet again serene as he nodded to display personal conviction - and Nefer felt herself shiver, the cool new frost on her beaker melting deep into her fingers.

"So of course we shall have to determine what brings on this... *condition,-*" Sinuhé eyed her Sire with the pacifying gleam of benign eyes that looked at odds with a curiously frugal smile, "-the Exalted One knows, after all, that any vision to do with the notion of twins, must not be deliberately overlooked. Indeed, the Watchéran knows as well as most that we cannot be too careful - not even if something is not mirrored by the Tapestry. All reports inform me that in many places the magic no longer operates within known perimeters, so perhaps it would not be inconceivable to discover some level of damage to the Tapestry as well?"

For a moment Nefer felt shocked but her father only waved a hand with dismissive candour as the certainty of his own convictions rolled off his presence.

"No that is not possible." He glanced at her new tutor with absolute confidence. "As you know, Commander Denarlin managed to extend warning. We of this realm stood protected and the Tapestry first and foremost. It cost us nine 7th Tiers and some of minor Talent also, but the wards held and though there are glitches to the occasional Weave, they are what you might call 'negligible'."

24

Sinuhé nodded, seemingly smooth features turning momentarily heavy under some grave burden. "Yes, it is true that the Sabén-Heshep people were relatively fortunate in their misfortune. Nine 7th Tier Spell-Weavers is a terrible loss - indeed, any life lost in this event was a terrible loss - yet without their sacrifice...!

"The people of Ostravah were not that privileged, I'm afraid - the Spell-Weavers that survived turned mad, so I judge the Watchéran understands that I had to consider the possibility that the Tapestry had not passed unscathed."

Nefer's Sire sighed, a flash of odd pain rushing his dark, polished features. "I cannot fault your logic Speaker Guardian, but we have taken every precaution; done extensive tests over the last centuries to ensure unpolluted continuity and nothing has been reported amiss. I am relieved to say that the Tapestry Weave remains unbroken."

Mirroring her Sire, Sinuhé sighing deeply, and the Watchéran held His visitor's blue gaze for a beat longer as if to offer reassurance, then he bowed his neck to the other man, all sombre respect as he seemingly capitulated. "You will of course do as you see fit in all aspects of this, Mshai. Now, as always."

Sinuhé stared a moment upon the swaying golden palms across the plaza, then back at the Watchéran. "Whatever happens I shall seek not to fuel existing problems - you have my word. To my relief, I cannot say I have felt any offset disturbance from the Tapestry, and unless my esteemed colleague has noted differently, I will not question the council's methods. The Vectors were always impeccable. Meticulous. I cannot think this will have changed."

Her Sire inclined his chin. "And my daughter?"

25

"We will go steady, of course." Sinu found her eyes. "She will not be stressed. I stand guarantee."

Nefer watched her Sire's appeasement expand like he'd been soothed by a charge of healing crystals scattered beneath the awning. "That would be appreciated. In many other respects, you will find her without equal. You see, she saw much before anyone could tell her: at only twenty turns of the Twin Rivers, she saw the arrival of my second wife five seasons before the occasion of our first meeting and she saw how her unborn half-sister would enter this realm without Affinity. She is not commonly wrong. She sees events, people, disasters - good Sinuhé, she sees the future of us all, and yet..."

Nefer opened her mouth to appeal to her father then but closed it again when she saw Sinuhé look at her with a peculiar expression. Her Sire did not believe her but something in the Mshai's face made her hopeful that he still did. *Maybe... just maybe...*

"In any event, I just hope we have time," Sinuhé injected, "I hope she is strong enough to bear this task."

"You will do well with her Mshai Sinuhé," He-Who-Is smiled, momentarily obscuring his lips as he raised his cup to take a slow sip before continuing, "My Sheriti knows much and has never been seen to shy from her duties. She knows of the Glorious Lands, about the War of Ages, about my Brothers and Sisters, about the Venzoian mistake, and she... she knows about the Upper Circle, if not the exact details surrounding the most recent developments. I would ask... that is: I would hope that perhaps you and the Flight of Fire might help her understand more."

"Perhaps a wise request good Watchéran - we shall attempt to oblige where possible, and yet..." Sinuhé paused for a blink - his face now also elegantly solemn - then continued, "Yet since she is still a child: perhaps I should not ask this of her? With matters as they are and with what we currently face, maybe...?"

"Hmm..." Her father's sublime lips twisted in a very Human manner. *He appeared rueful.*

In all of Nefer's short life, many strange things had already happened but along with all else, she was more than a little taken aback at this continuous intimate show of uncertainty, both from her Sire as well as from a man she had only just met. Yet for everything, something about her was pleasing Sinuhé immensely though and her Sire was complimented - she saw that, too.

"Mshai Sinuhé," her father's dark features altered, the tone boding no objection, "We are at war. You seek aide. You seek a 'miracle' - a revelation by which to shed light upon the past, present and future. Nefer will help you - as you will help her. If there is something un-revealed - she'll guide you. In spite the Amalgamations - *that is* her gift! With council and support, it may be honed beyond these random visions to search the particulars as required. But she is young; untested. She'll need the guidance to do well and in this only you will do! Not the Flight of Fire! Not the Chief of Vectors! Only you - for as long as you can spare!"

Clutching the small effigy of the panther between the once-more warm fingers of her left hand, Nefer'Kemnebit stayed quiet, sensing that this was another of those moments where the value of her Affinity was stated for adult purposes. And that the two men might not agree.

However, her tutor simply nodded his understanding at her Sire's words: as if they made the most perfectly painful sense to him. Then he sighed with a hint of resignation and in recognition of agreement.

27

"Lady Lotus, Ankh'Sheriti-Nefer'Kemnebit, most precious Jewel of Knowledge, Daughter of He-Who-Is, Sheshem'Kufunar, unfortunately, we do not have much time. Your 'Birthright' is about to truly blossom and it will be magnificent, but there is a danger too and we mustn't let it claim you or the route back will be slow and painful. Yet would you be brave and help us?"

Nefer smiled. A wide set of teeth. *Yes.*

Sinuhé seemed regretful but then he relented with a smile of his own, also wide: also enough to highlight his Human aspects once more. "Now with your Sire's blessing, we will go directly to visit the Council of Historic Preservation, just as we will seek out the Chief of Vectors to alert him of your newest vision-"

"But he will not listen!" she burst out, eyes flying from father and back. "He-"

"My dearest Sheriti," Sinuhé admonished, "one should never interrupt another. It is rude beyond measure. That said, however, there may be times..."

And here her mentor's eyes rolled to her Sire's, "That is to say, there may be times where leniency may be granted, as is the case with these 'supposed' rouge visions. After all, we do appear unable to find any transcripts of the event that saw the Balance of Justice fall from our midst too - and surely the Tapestry should have been Weaving to document this."

Her father didn't move, but Sinu continued, "Somewhere, somehow there is a thing or two out of sync and we might as well strike hard at the centre of the matter, lest we be faced with more 'pleasantries' as the power the Veils begin to fade."

Understanding what was about to happen, a burst of elation shot through Nefer - still, her joy dimmed almost instantly. Her father did

28

not look happy and as Nefer watched with dwindling optimism, He-Who-Is stared with perfectly expressionless features at her tutor.

Something unspoken seemed to pass between the two men. Then...

"Well, that is indeed a wise precaution," the Watchéran allowed after yet a beat, "And you will do as you must, Guardian. But Nefer's odd visions about these twins cannot accurately reflect the future. They must not! Imagine for a moment if one might accurately predict the course of the-"

Abruptly He-Who-Is broke off. His entire bearing hinting at denial, his tone grew firm, "No, Mshai Sinuhé, Nefer is gifted but these particular visions - though detailed they might be...? They... they cannot herald truth! The Tapestry is silent. Other Far Seers foretell of no such calamity brewing - and for good reason, I suspect! What she is 'predicting' simply cannot come to pass. And if it did? Well, if it did: where would such development leave us all? Would it be the end? No old friend, the Tapestry would throw us the signs and warn us to prepare. It has ever been so!"

"Perhaps," Sinuhé allowed, "but both you and I are old enough to know that sometimes - just sometimes - the impossible becomes reality. In any event, no harm will come from investigating all avenues. Like I said: I shall not seek to alienate nor discredit, and like you said: the sooner we straighten this, the better. I have my reluctant, if impeccably sharp, 'research assistant'. This will be no burden and I am sure he will soon put our fears to rest, besides."

As though they'd just shared a private jest, now He-Who-is smiled like a smug conspirator, a sight most peculiar to Nefer. "Yes, I believe you are correct - at least on that last score. *He* is not pleased to have his 'abilities' go wasted now, is he? But then again, I guess he never was. To us all, he alone gives the Elvern people a bad name!"

"Indeed,-" Sinuhé's smile tightened a fraction, "-yet heed your words regardless. The Flight of Fire owns good moments too! Just because he's lost the Sight, you must not forget who he is! Kindly show him the respect he's owed, even if it pains you."

Nefer'Kemnebit stared in surprise as her Sire bowed His head as though contrite, "Yes, Mshai Sinuhé. Of course. How could I ever forget?" He looked up. "I owe him much; owe you all much. I will not forget. Please do as you see appropriate. Sheriti is now your concern but keep me appraised. She is dear to me. Very dear."

"As the Esteemed One wishes, so it shall be done," Sinuhé replied with a respectful lilt but Nefer'Kemnebit noted that her tutor did not bow as any other person might have done to have spoken so harshly-direct at her Sire. *They'd talked of the Upper Circle, and though she was unfamiliar with the true names of the Maker's Avatars, she wondered-*

"Mshai Sinuhé, one request if I might," her Sire's voice cut through her intrigue.

"Esteemed One, if I am able..." her tutor acquiesced.

"Is there news of the Artefact?" her Sire enquired, casual but with concern in His dark eyes.

"None!" Sinuhé frowned, four deep lines scoring paths like dry river beds across his forehead. "We will look of course but without the Twins, I believe it futile. If a shard is indeed present in your lands, I do not think that it will reveal itself unduly. When the Twins arrive, however...

"Yes, when the Twins arrive." her Sire concurred with an uncharacteristic furrow to mirror her tutor's. Then, almost as an afterthought, he queried, "And yet if any clues as to its whereabouts should materialize, you will inform me?"

"Upon my word," Sinuhé promised without reserve. Then, turning to Nefer'Kemnebit, he interrupted her musings in earnest, "Dearest Heart, are you ready? We will see the Chief of Vectors presently. It will be a busy day I fear, but he must at the very least give us leeway for consideration for there is something here that warrants attention. Something serious - and he must grasp the truth of this, surely. Our work is started; there are things that we must investigate and clarify; puzzles to solve. Perhaps, dear Nefer, the place for us to start after the Council, would be the Tapestry Scrolls? Sounds fair?"

Nefer knew she probably ought to answer, but it seemed she needn't concern herself. With barely a nod for her Sire, Sinuhé straightened with an energetic flourish to pull her from the cushioned seat with a most-assuming tug at the pleated fabric of her tunic.

Setting the beaker down, she scrambled to comply though in slight uproar.

For moments, she half-expected her Sire to order the man seized and thrown to his knees before them both at this all-too-familiar conduct, but yet again her father never moved nor uttered a word of displeasure. Instead, He simply made a silent gesture and then she and Sinuhé were off, hastening across the warm, white tiles of the courtyard as though late for the daily Hour of Redemption.

Breathless with the turn of events, uncertain still of what exactly had happened just moments before, Nefer'Kemnebit, oldest living daughter of He-Who-Is, simply followed.

Eyeing the old man as he marched with purpose, she tried to find a word or gesture to suit, but there were none. Sinuhé's complete break with custom left her mute and she obediently moved in the

31

wake of her new mentor's billowing toga - if not the happy puppy, then nevertheless also not the unhappy servant unable to resist argument.

As it happened, a small but growing part of her soon revelled in the development. Gone were the measured glide and the graceful appearance as she half-walked, half-trotted behind this strange Suten Hamu who was seemingly above any normal order. Fear that her Mama should hear of this conduct made her cringe to be sure, and yet a small seed of excitement that had begun to grow in her belly just couldn't be ignored. *Her new tutor might be strange, but he was not like the others either; somehow, Sinuhé sensed the truth of her visions and he was willing to believe her - and that in spite her age! Could he truly sway the Council without more endless hours of questions?*

Nefer'Kemnebit knew a tiny smile tugged at her mouth at the thought. *If he could, now that would be a thing worth seeing - and sooner rather than later too, it seemed!*

Setting this fast pace, they quickly drew close to one of the wide door-openings leading back into the main Complex. With the folding screens currently thrown back to allow what small breeze there might be to flow into the shadow beyond, access was easy - and never pausing they proceeded under the giant maze-adorned lintel and down a wide corridor.

They had not ventured far though, when a sudden but small prick inside Nefer's hand made her gasp in surprise. Realising that she'd once again been clasping the small black figurine unduly tight, she reflexively opened her palm to check what damage she might have caused herself, and...

32

The sight that met her eyes, stopped her dead mid-step. Dumb-struck, she stared, then blinked. *Once... twice.*

In the palm of her hand the little statue moved, tilting its head, and...

Licking its tiny mouth just once as it glared at her without blinking, the former figuring expelled a tiny breath: very... very much alive.

Nefer'Kemnebit blinked again.

As real as the soft paws and sharp tiny claws that dug a minuscule fraction into the top layer of her skin, the cat flicked its tiny long tail as though to proclaim and establish that she definitely wasn't having yet another vision and Nefer felt her eyes go round. *This was magic beyond scope; beyond anything, she'd ever known. This-*

From the corner of her eye, she sensed movement as her new mentor belatedly paused to check in response to the small exclamation she'd made, but even as she sensed his concern turn to light relief, Nefer could look only at the small cat residing in the palm of her hand.

Somehow, impossibly, it had become a creature of flesh and blood but almost she could not believe it. How... how was her tutor allowed?

With a last flicker of the end of its tail, the cat finally broke off its lingering golden-green stare of imagined indignant slight and began instead to groom its short sleek fur with aloof eagerness.

"Well my Lotus, looks like you might have been squashing her a little too tightly there, but no harm's done." Sinuhé smiled as he arrived back at her side and looked down. With a small sound of approval, he exclaimed, "Well she's pretty, Dear One! Oh, and she's got the same colour eyes as you, methinks!"

Nefer'Kemnebit gasped again, eyes rushing to Sinuhé's but never lingering long before the cat drew them back. *Her tutor's matter-of-fact attitude did nothing to help her recover as she continued to stare at the tiny miracle in her hand.*

Questions brewing, somehow she diverted her gaze to him and found her voice. "But how... how is this possible?!"

Sinuhé smiled, an edge of youthful mischief flattering his face.

Tapping the left side of his nose with one long index finger as he neglected to answer outright, he volunteered instead a little advice, "Nefer'Kemnebit, now hear my words: hear me and remember! Just because she is little, it does not mean that she has not got the teeth to bite or the claws to scratch. Nor does it mean that she hasn't a voice worth hearing, for that matter.

"Sheriti dear, never make the mistake of assuming that just because of size, she won't possess the exact same instincts and wits of her much larger counterparts; as with the majority of things, most are not what they seem, so let her be a perfect reminder of this complex - and let's go meet with the Council."

"But... But..." Nefer'Kemnebit was still speechless but her tutor's words seemed wise somehow, so she nodded, taking her eyes back to the wonder in her palm and the tiny perfectly-formed black panther paused its grooming and emitted a purr. Then nonchalantly ignoring their attention as only a cat is able, it snuggled down, easily curling into a small ball at the centre of her hand.

"Remember, Dear Heart, she might only be small, but just like you, she is very special. If her growl be but slight, only a fool ignores her at his peril. And, so it is with you. One should save judgement, before getting to know the strength of her. Guard her well and she will grow with you in more ways than you can imagine."

34

Like a loving uncle reassuring an uncertain youngster, Sinuhé then patted her forehead with the flat of his hand and turned from her, absent-mindedly wiping his palm on the lower-most pleats of his belted toga as he continued down the corridor: somehow oblivious to the now-lingering traces of her costly gold-paints upon his pale-bleached garment.

"But… bu-" Voice failing, Ankh'Sheriti-Nefer'Kemnebit, esteemed Best-Loved Daughter of He-who-Is and the Best-Loved Suten Himé, First-Queen Tanafriti-Nafretiri, could only gape in open-mouthed astonishment.

No one had ever dared touch her head with such void of care or concern before. Ti'Anakit'Suh's Affinity was strong - yet Sinuhé had just rubbed her head as though the runes had been but some sort of delicate beautiful decoration. *No one did that! No one!*

Still, fact remained that her new tutor had irrevocably ruined the painted symbols - there could be no question from the evidence on his hands - and now his garments; indeed, he should presently lie comatose on the floor, or else be writhing in pain from the sting of conjured poisons, but he didn't!

Nefer felt like crying, but not because the Benedictions appeared to have lacked the intended effect. She was still in public! What would people think?

For a moment she felt as indignant as the small cat had been upon being squeezed, and almost she was about to change her favourable opinion of the old man, but then her eyes fell back on the tiny feline resting in her hand. With a subtle purr, it stared right back at her, gleaming faceted eyes mysteriously inscrutable…

Nefer's emotions wobbled.

"Just like you - remember! Just like you!" Her tutor's voice carried back along the corridor, jolting her to look up. *Just like me...*

Already a goodly length down the pale-stoned passage, Sinuhé strolled on, full of purpose.

"Now will you be keeping the Council waiting for long, Dear Heart?" he enquired over one surprisingly square shoulder with a lightness fraught by suppressed humour, "Or should I just tell them that you are presently too occupied to visit? Recall, if you would: the future is a-waiting."

Nefer's lips twitched. Just once. *The pouting bee stings her third sister would tease end the smile grew.* She might only be young in years, but she had already experienced a lifetime of events and this... *well, this was now! And it was hers!*

Sighing at the miniature creature in her hand, she gave in with nothing more than a resigned shrug. *This was beyond her, and the excitement was dancing back...*

Cradling her fingers protectively around the panther, careful not to squeeze it now, she started forward to catch up with her bizarre tutor. There was something about him that had her wondering at secret things - and she'd not forgotten how her Sire had dealt with him: she'd heard them refer to the Flight of Fire and the Balance of Justice - both Avatar names - and perhaps-

The truth of it hit her like the power of a vision.

Sinuhé was of the Upper Circle. He had to be: the signs were there. The Maker's touch on his skin, the silent power in him, the authority, her Sire's deference...

Nefer shook her head, a snake of wonder twisting her insides. She wasn't sure she understood the reasons for his presence but there was something different in the air: something almost tangible; a taste of change. Her father had told Sinuhé that she did not know much about the Upper Circle, yet she knew enough. *Knew that it belonged to Alérathnar the Maker's Chosen: to the Ascended; the Re-born; the Ancients...*

She knew the Millennium was neigh - *of course, just what one of the esteemed Ancients could possibly need from her, she did not understand* - however, if he could help the Chief of Vectors see matters her way, she would not shy from offering her new tutor whatever he asked of her.

The twin must not die; the Blue-haired Mshai must not betray them: it would kill the other twin: mind and heart - and then the Age of Dust would be as unavoidable as the swarms of autumn locust, except it would devour every last scrap of life down to every final drop of water and magic, leaving nothing for the future but sorrow and death. *But Sinuhé had Power. And he believed her. Of all the things she had seen, this had never been in the crystals. Which gave her hope...*

Angemar's Mistress

But he couldn't know her, could he?

Solancei del'Isthalani Calverhana told herself she hadn't recognized Angemar Cillario's voice earlier for the very good reason that she'd simply never met this man before! *Starved prisoner, dishevelled or not, there was nothing even remotely familiar about him and she would have remembered someone with high cheekbones like that, wouldn't she?*

She warred at her bottom lip with her teeth, somehow unable to sever eye contact as she did her meagre calculations. *Sadly, she wasn't sure if her ignorance mattered.* Simaro would already be making deductions of his own. They'd be formed on speculation and imaginings, of course, but once he thought himself on the right track, he'd be unlikely to believe words to the contrary, no matter how wrong his reasoning. *And Gods be good, there could well be a hundred reasons why Angemar was reacting like he recognized her. A hundred and more! Fleck, yes he could by chance have seen her with the Princess, or he could have been a spectator at another jackal fight, or he could be a spy...*

Solancei pulled her gaze from the prisoner with a slight narrowing of her the eyes so to warn him against all and nothing. Simaro was straightening his tunic and belt but he still looked in disarray: as if the lavenders had not pressed and folded his clothes appropriately. *It was mildly gratifying.*

In spite everything, Solancei smiled inwardly. The sight he presented should have found her dropping comments of mockery – *Gods, he looked much less the courtier now and more the rowdy tavern jouster!* – but Angemar's reaction was stuck in her mind,

38

boiling up her unease. *Fleck, the last thing she needed was some loony moon-brain yammering on about something he thought to be true just to curry favour, or just to escape his chains!*

Spearing Angemar with another look, her eyes spoke the caution her mouth could not. His black gaze had not strayed and riveted thus to her person, he did not even appear to have blinked.

Solancei pulled the Link tighter. After the scrap, the prisoner's left eye was slightly bruised but there was a hint of desperation in his demeanour suddenly - nothing to do with the swords they'd aimed at his chest or his sorry predicament - but rather something that hinted of madness and just a fraction of... *of disbelief?*

"I have neglected this inevitable duty of mine for too long,-" Simaro spoke up with a touch of aloof noble vanity as he left his clothes alone to concentrate fully on Angemar again. "-and thus I consider this small 'debacle' my own fault."

"Well thank fleck for that!" Angemar grated simply, finally shifting to pin his attention to his jailor, though not in meek surrender as one might have expected after his defeat: Solancei saw his eyes rest briefly, but hungrily, upon Simaro's dagger before drifting once more.

Tugging a few times at the scabbard's frog, absently re-settling his sword at a better angle, Simaro simply sighed to himself and for the briefest of moments, something flickered deep in Angemar eyes: a glimmer of zeal, perhaps; something lethal.

Then he rolled his gaze back to her face and Solancei swallowed a gasp at the almost serene expression now offered. Somehow she couldn't bear the quality of pressure in that one look and she blinked rapidly, hiding emotions.

"Now you had your little revolt, Cillario: bravo." Simaro wiped a hand across the small cut in his lower lip as if he wished to smooth it away, and seemed annoyed to be reminded that the injury was still there.

The quality of his tone running tart, he carried on, "You did not achieve what you wanted, I imagine, but still: take heart that you got as far as you did. It should make you feel better, yes?"

In response, Angemar heaved a deep breath - for the first time that Solancei was aware - looking at the swords and hands that pressed him against the wall.

"Better..." His voice trailed off as his eyes wandered to Simaro. "I will feel better only when I see your rotting corpse torn apart by the creatures that crawl the night and lurk in the shadows in-between. This true, however, for now I will take pride in the knowledge that for once you have verily erred."

Angemar flashed Simaro an eerie expression that might have passed for a smile in a nightmare, then lowered his gaze as his shoulders slowly started shaking.

On fine cue, the soldiers looked instantly uncertain and for a beat Solancei thought the prisoner was going to sub-come to another round of those tremors that seemed to afflict him so randomly, but Angemar raised his head quick as a sparrow then - the eyes drilling into Simaro, suddenly brimming with a touch of chilling madness. *A dry, jaundiced laughter escaped the prisoner, polluting the air with choler.*

"And you find this amusing, why?" Simaro enquired, evidently untouched by Angemar's behaviour, yet clasping both hands around his sword belt as if to brace himself, and the prisoner's grin widened.

"It is amusing, you bastard,-" Angemar's laughter smothered in a blink underneath an uncompromising flare of fey madness that seemed to burn in his eyes without fuel, "-because for the first time I see the beginning!

"The beginning?" Simaro repeated, flatly.

"The beginning," Angemar confirmed, raising his head. Barring his teeth at Simaro in a switchblade smile, he said, "The beginning! The beginning, yes. And the End. The beginning..."

The feral smile vanished as though stolen by a passing spirit. "Oh Lord of Shite and Death, how sweet it is to know that you have no idea! No idea, no idea, no idea."

Angemar ripped his gaze from Simaro, suddenly and abruptly, his good eye losing the odd, shimmering focus in favour of a strangely faraway gleam as he centred his attention back on Solancei. *It felt eerie.*

"Cillario!" She heard Simaro bark, "Cillario, snap back!"

The prisoner only shook his head. "Ar verdan narah!"

Disconcerted, Solancei's mind was just a heartbeat slower than usual in translating the words of the ancient language he'd just spoken, but then it came to her: *'He sees nothing!'*

Surprise made her swallow hard as questions flooded her mind in a beat, but Angemar's eyes seemed to bore into her very core, halting her.

For now, sharpened focus had replaced his far-away look but the uncanny transition was sending a shiver down her spine - not in fear this time, but rather in queer surprise to hear him utter words of a language that was commonly considered dead anywhere but to a handful of dusty scholars at the Etruian Library.

41

"Ar verdan narah. Portarda narah tempar," Angemar continued. *'He sees nothing. You need carry fear of nothing,'* her mind translated, quicker now, as he carried on, "Stara ben quia Mahcia voi domar vitalionan; toi seir- ugh"

Angemar's head snapped sideways as Simaro backhanded him with a snarl that twisted his cool features with hard distaste.

"Now why this? Why these lengthy tirades of words that no one speaks?" Simaro was fierce and impatient. "May Arbar'Chi's plough find your backside, man! You test my patience and bore my guest. I warn you just once to desist, or you will know regret, you mush-head fool!"

"Oh?" Angemar's eyes were a little slow in focussing on the man before him, but as he regained control, he offered Simaro an insolent grin, "Oh is that a promise then?"

Simaro growled and moved like a striking viper to snatch a hank of the prisoner's hair, forcing him hard against the rock so that the guards had to shift hastily to reorganise their blades.

Angemar's face sawed in half on a smile; faces now inches apart, Simaro drew his fancy dagger with fecund warning and Angemar raised his chin a fraction. *Inviting...*

From her vantage point, Solancei saw Simaro's features turned pristine and cold. Temper rattling its chains of confinement, she recognised the expression and condemned Simaro yet again. *Whether this fellow prisoner thought he knew her or not, he was still sick and Simaro was making it worse. She might not be a Wise Woman, but this Angemar Cillario certainly needed one! And he'd just spoken to her in High Armearan...*

"Please stop it!" she petitioned Simaro, pulling forward a little against the guards who still held onto her as if the danger had not passed.

One breath...

"That man is clearly out of his mind!" She scrambled her courage, continuing, "You cannot punish those who draw each breath with half their sight upon the world *Beyond.* If you do, you damage yourself in the eyes of the Gods." *I don't give a fig for the Gods and your standing, but it might give you pause, and...*

Still clasping Angemar's hair Simaro looked across, meeting her eyes.

"And what would you know of such things, grey-eyes? You turned your back on your chance to serve!" Simaro's cool gaze narrowed and she saw Angemar behind him, suddenly with wide eyes imploring her...? *Imploring to stay silent?*

Solancei looked away. "I know... maybe... maybe nothing."

Simaro expelled a breath. He made it sound as if he was balancing somewhere between mockery and laughter but he released Angemar with a disgusted grimace all the same then, giving the prisoner's head one last push in derision before sauntering towards her instead.

"The man is mad as those lost to the moonlight and spirits, yes I know," Simaro agreed whilst contemplating his dagger and directing a casual flick of his chin in Angemar's direction, "And he speaks in tongues and mad confusion: parts of the drivel he sprouts might be considered traceable to the King's Tongue, but mostly it's just tripe nonsense even if it may seem to ring like poetry of the Gods. It gets in your ears though, and plays with your mind, turning you half-mad

43

for even trying to guess. He calls it High Armearan, but everyone knows that is a lost language."

And so it makes you feel inferior, you illiterate oaf! Solancei sucked in a deep breath to keep the words back and cast the prisoner a quick glance. He was mumbling something to himself under his breath whilst looking at the two of them; something she could not make out, maybe but for the smooth syllables; something in the same language as before.

Fervent as his lips moved with a mantra-like, avid flow, Solancei wondered if Angemar could perhaps be praying - except it seemed an unlikely possibility for the Gods did not deign to offer attention in the darkness; indeed, in Solancei's experience, *they* listened only to the sound of valuables offered and gold plates stacked!

Yet Angemar paid such considerations no mind and she listened harder.

'Carry no fear. All will be well.' - she made out then: the same words he'd spoken before - *But why?*

"You see?" Simaro prompted with a shrug, but Angemar's eyes seemed to burn her and she shook herself.

"I... ehh... I...

"He is not well!" she reiterated, struggling not to mull over the meaning of the prisoner's successive words. *Something about magic...?* She could be wrong though and wished that Simaro had let him finish.

Turning her eyes from the prisoner, seeing again the flicker of madness rotate like windmills in his dark eyes, she wondered if he even knew what he'd been saying.

"Oh I know he is unwell." Simaro threw her a languid smile that made the hairs on her arms stand on end. "That said, I did not

44

bargain for all the potent twaddle he seems to sprout, that much I'll readily confess. Mayhap I was foolish for thinking he could lend aide?"

The pale-haired man shrugged again as if it didn't matter one way or another and reached out to calmly claim her arm from the closest guard, "Perhaps there is no choice but-"

"Take your filthy hands off My Lady of the Light!" Angemar injected over him, his voice cold warning and cultured disdain.

Startled, Simaro paused for a beat, almost letting go of her, then he seemed to gather his aplomb, "My-lady-of-the-what-now?"

Angemar shifted against his guards and tried to speak but they wrestled him back, preventing him, and Simaro issued a cold huff, dismissing him in favour of Solancei.

"I guess by your expression that you also find yourself wondering what the man is speaking of?"

Solancei didn't have to pretend. "Yes, he... he makes little sense."

She peered at Simaro through her lashes, insides turning in alarm lest he should choose not to believe her, but at least the Veranto kept her heart steady.

"My Lady!" Angemar insisted, pushing against the men again, risking cuts or worse as swords wavered whilst they forced him back. Sounding desperate he ignored them, "My Lady! Mistress! Please listen... *listen!*"

Spilling forth a flood of words in High Armearan, Angemar flung himself forward as if he meant to reach her and Simaro - the flood rapidly becoming a river of sentences pouring out faster and faster, even as the men wrestled to fling him back into line, pushing him till his words became cut by sounds of staggered breaths and the oaths of their struggle.

45

It hardly mattered. Solancei felt herself staring in slack-mouthed wonder. *What he was saying made no sense. She understood what he is saying: it was a little backwards - or maybe it only sounded thus because he spoke a formal tense - but it did not matter. None of it made any sense to her.*

She blinked in confusion, her mind spinning as she wavered, attempting to decide who to focus on - the prisoner, or Simaro.

Artefacts of importance; boundaries; names of lands or provinces she'd never heard of before; names of people; of commanding officers - or Marshalls, if her translation wasn't completely off...

Solancei shook her head imperceptibly. Angemar was speaking to her of these things as if he thought she should know about them... *and understand!*

But she didn't. Or else she was simply not as good at deciphering High Armearan as she'd once been led to believe...

Between cussing and breaths, Angemar spoke up again, but Solancei wanted him to stop. *Gods, what was this 'vengeance of magic'? A thing, or a book, or a curse, or something else entirely? And what did this 'light bearer' title mean? He kept addressing her with the word 'heragistra' - or Mistress - as though he owed her fealty or some such, and what was the supposed warning about 'the shards of all and nothing'?*

With a sense of despair welling up, she felt herself beginning to speak over his mad ramblings. Angemar was undoubtedly as lost as a Priest of Osari'Chi released after his year of solitude and prayers - for a beat, she'd been sure he'd been saying something about a wedding too... *her flecking own!*

46

"You are right," she told Simaro, not understanding why she should feel so sad suddenly, "the man talks the words of an addled mind. I don't understand him. What… what would you do with him?"

"Mistress! No!" Angemar shouted as if in denial, but with an echo of despair, "No, you must listen to me! I implore you! You must! I would lend you strength!"

Solancei swallowed but kept her gaze squarely on Simaro. Her duplicity cut her, but she did not comprehend the meanings of the things Angemar had reamed off and there was no point in stirring Simaro's intrigue by admitting that she knew the language and the words, when not the context.

Simaro gave the man a dark look, his brows furrowing. "He's no longer fit for anything but the butcher's block. This is not the outcome I'd hoped for when I took you down here, but after a fashion, I suppose he will still serve a purpose."

The butcher's block… a purpose? As if an animal afflicted with an incurable blight.

"Let him go," Solancei suggested and felt her heart thump harder in her chest, "Set him free, and I would tell you what you want, I swear. Other information… information that my origins in New Wood cannot account for."

That caught Simaro by surprise, she saw. Clearly such a bargaining plea had been the last thing he'd expected from her, and still-

"No, Mistress, no!" Angemar's voice rose up, pulling her attention to him as he implored, "Don't do this! He will use you! Don't let him! All will be well, if only-"

A sharp punch cut Angemar's desperate outburst off as the guard on his left moved to silence him permanently, but Simaro raised a

47

hand to forestall further abuse, giving her a sly look as he slowly let the arm sink again.

"This man is a crazed wrack - worth nothing before he came here, worth nothing now that he's about to leave! He cannot hope for a future, grey-eyes! Why would you care to help him?"

Solancei felt his grip on her arm intensify slightly for emphasis and it made her question her own sanity. *She'd defended Angemar. Why? Because he was mad and couldn't help himself? Because she did not want another human being to become just 'meat and bones' to the nightmares across that rift? Because she was a wretch that could not stand idle to spite her own flesh...?* As a matter of fact, she was not sure - but no one should treat a prisoner like Simaro had done Angemar. *The man was sick. Mentally and physically.*

Solancei drew a breath to fortify herself. *Iambre, I am sorry...*

"I understand it might mean nothing to you perhaps," she began, finding Angemar's dark eyes. He seemed serene as they shared a strange, silent communique - but she also saw him blink in pain just once, his gaze glittering with some kind of appeal or denial or both.

Resolutely she said, "To me, he is still a person. Under Crown-Law, he still has rights. Even here. So set him free and you will have what you want. Be it what it may, I will bend to your demands."

Even as Solancei spoke, the words stripped off moisture to become ashes in her mouth but she did not try to rescind them, even if for a moment she thought she might choke as her throat seemed to close up of its own accord as though in objection.

"Well, well now..." Simaro let go of her arm and turned towards Angemar. He seemed pleased. "Let's see what I can do then."

Gesturing to his men that they should let the prisoner stand, Simaro pointed his dagger at him, demanding attention. "Angemar...

48

seems some remnant of your charming personality still holds a sifter of power then. And what a fortuitous thing that grey-eyes here appears to harbour a hidden soft spot for rejects too. Perhaps…? Well, perhaps this might be your lucky day after all."

Angemar only grunted. As the soldiers left him be, the man seemed oblivious as he simply stood there, crooked of frame, slumped in stature, as though internal burdens claimed his strength.

A soft quiver raced through his body, jostling the chains. Almost she expected him to look at her then, but as it were, Angemar did not attempt to make eye contact again, though for a moment he did stir to expel a hard, spluttering cough.

It terminated in a sound that might have passed for half a laugh of derision - dry and void of mirth, but for the hint of desolate self-contempt.

"Lucky day, you say?" he mumbled under his breath, voice barely audible, "Lucky day?" Angemar haltingly lifted his chin to stare directly at his captor. With an odd sheen in the eye, he repeated, "Lucky day?"

Sounding unhinged in a way that made a chill flow down Solancei's back, Angemar issued another sound what might have passed for a brittle laugh. "Yes… my lucky day! Oh but you have no idea, traitor; no idea! Kira'Cha you bitch, go palm your sister! This lucky day… mine… yes, lucky. So very, very lucky."

Simaro appraised the shackled man, a peculiar inquisitive expression forming on his face.   "Lord Angemar, you are droll as ever. Is the 'medicine' wearing off, my friend?"

Shivering, a rapid succession of violent tremors rattled the prisoner, each breath leaving his chest in short rapid burst until he seemed to be panting with anger, or hurt, or perhaps even both. It made Solancei sick. Once more, there was an intense look in the stranger's deep eyes. He did not move, but-

He wants to kill Simaro, she thought, *but he knows he can't. He is too sick and he knows it and he hates it! Will I be the same?*

She fought the urge to ask Simaro what the man's crime had been; fought the urge to ask what Simaro had done to the poor prisoner and what he meant by 'medicine', cowardly fearing that she knew the answer, to at least the latter question.

"Lucky day indeed, traitor!" Angemar rattled off, deep voice turned gravelly from pain - yet though the tremors seemed to quiver through him as though he was shivering from a fever, his eyes found hers past Simaro's frame, something bright in their depths growing.

"Lucky, lucky day take my pain away!" Angemar chanted like a zealot priest in a jarring, simple sing-song tone, "He will never know, but for the errors, he will pay. Yes... pay he will. Dearly, dearly! Lucky, lucky day, so this is how it begins then. Begins... and ends... and begins..."

Simaro snorted softly to himself, voicing another comment of demented value, but Solancei didn't really listen. As he muttered the same words over and over, grotesquely, Angemar reminded her of her old astrology tutor in the way that he'd fluctuate between lucidity one moment, only then to get randomly lost in a thought or theory - perhaps brought to mind by nothing more than a word or a gesture - before he'd turn a blunt finger her way and demand an answer to something utterly unrelated.

"... lucky, never know... never..." The prisoner's near-reverent tirade petered off. As if he was suddenly verbally and physically spent he did not seem to note as one final quiver rocked him, then left him strangely still.

50

This is grotesque indeed, Solancei thought, *grotesque and utterly unnerving.* To her, the atmosphere was as eerie as the effects of an iceberg coming apart in one of the great spring-melts of her former home: the enormous chunks dropping off into the ocean with violent splashes, accompanied it would seem, by the keening songs of mourning spirits. Afterwards, the waters would be as still as a grave site - as smoothly serene as the Queen's own face - without a wind to stir the surface, and the silence as deep and cold as the iceberg had been tall and majestic. It was that same kind of strange feeling that seemed to rip through her now as she watched Angemar take a halting step forward.

A real sense of before and after seemed to linger in the atmosphere: the sort that left a person feeling very small and powerless to influence the bigger events in nature. Right from the now-quiet Hyatts, to Simaro's oddly swaying disposition, to Angemar's bizarre, changing behaviour, somehow she got the feeling that she was the only sane person left standing and even that was a notion rapidly unravelling. This could possibly be the strangest day she'd ever experienced - a day that seemed it could not possibly get any worse - but who was she kidding? *Things could always get worse. Usually, when things got worse, it was heralded by someone dying, and she had a really itchy feeling about this!*

"Could we just get this over with?" Solancei petitioned Simaro. "You will take the bargain, yes?"

Simaro eyed Angemar, then offered her a smile that seemed to cut his face as though sliced by a sabre. "Milady has my word, this deal is done. Now Angemar, you-"

"Thank you, My Lady!" In utter ignorance of what Simaro might have been about to say, Angemar breathed the sounds softly, the syllables barely reaching her though he shifted a step forward.

Simaro's mouth shut with an audible click of teeth, and Solancei had a wild moment to wonder what would happen next when Angemar slowly raised his head - doddering, jagged moves riding him like an old man.

Yet he seemed 'sane' once more now, a surprisingly heartfelt echo of sentiment filling the dark gaze that captured her to the spot and she felt a queer kind of kinship with the man as the liquid black of those now-lucid eyes bore into hers.

She heard Simaro sigh but he did not interfere as the prisoner hobbled nearer, continuing, "And thank you for this brave intervention. It is both noble and bravely done, but... but I fear, completely in vain; nevertheless..."

Solancei started shaking her head in denial of his words, but before she could add voice to objection, he made a gesture with one hand that set the chain rattling and she fell silent.

Angemar drew a heavy breath and looked down on her features, the unexpected curve of a smile gracing the face behind the beard.

"And nevertheless-" he reiterated, "-a condemned man thanks every kindness he can get, even when his day grows short, and so My Lady-"

He paused to let a tiny shiver pass, then sucked in breath and looked her in the eye, "And so, you have my heartfelt thanks, now and always!"

Rendered mute, Solancei could only stare. The prisoner's words were strangely eloquent: polite with a touch of old-fashioned flair in spite of his dreadful circumstances and his lack of accent definitely did not hide even a hint of the common Imkarahian soft slur.

So perhaps he was of Kerikonese origins instead? It would account for the cheekbones, but... but no. The Kerikonese were typically thought of as 'self-centred', and they were not fond of leaving their own province either. *They'd help each other like brothers, but walk over a dying stranger...*

Solancei knew her face portrayed her questions - and didn't care. *Perhaps he truly thought her someone else. Was that why he seemed so protective?*

Unable to puzzle it out, she was eerily aware of Simaro's eyes: settled upon their every move like Arbar'Chi Himself trailing in her shadow, present and steely, learning, deducting. It was impossible to imagine what he thought, but she could hazard a guess; her mind was screaming to work out the enigma presented by Angemar, but suddenly she was glad that she'd been prudent enough to bend her neck to custom and wear that ruddy statutory veil throughout most official arrangements. *Fleck, Angemar might indeed have seen her at court. There were always hundreds of visitors; he could have been anyone in a score; anyone in a hundred! And yet?*

And yet, she still thought it not the case. It was her job to be observant. Iambre's court sessions, council hearings and appearances could be lengthy affairs, often boring too; to pass the time she'd look at people: look at their expressions and reactions and the way their bodies and faces might sometimes say one thing and their mouths another.

She licked her lips. "You are... I mean, this is-"

"My Lady, waste not words." Angemar smiled, allowing her to catch a glimpse of the winsome person he might once have been. It silenced her even as he added, "For a moment whilst forever passes, allow me just the time to look at you."

Look? Feeling strange, she only nodded, expecting Simaro to cut this tiny audience short, but it seemed he was still intrigued and nothing happened.

It stimulated more questions - still, Solancei stayed quiet then. *Not only did Angemar seem genuine, he had also addressed her as 'Heragistra': the word for 'Mistress' in High Armearan. Was his act simply nothing more than good manners and curtsey?*

In her present state, it seemed an unlikely explanation. From a Kerikonese man it seemed an impossible word to use for someone who stank and looked little better than a sell-sword fallen on hard times, and since the Imkarahians were not known for their polite manners or educated consideration...?

For a beat it struck her that perhaps he was someone, pretending to be someone else. *Like herself.* But under such duress, was the prisoner really that accomplished? *Was he a master at the game of Smoke and mirrors? To mask a truth best never told?*

If she chose to believe it so, it only left more questions. It was a bouncing-in-the-bog type of demented, but she'd heard the slight infliction of respect in his voice when he addressed her: the kind of regard that simple, casual politeness did not measure up to, particularly between two random prisoners of supposedly random origins. *And besides, the title 'Heragistra' was not just an antiquated term of respect either.* If she recalled her lessons correctly - *and she thought she did; Gods they corrected her often enough to begin with: over and over until her misguided translations became a thing of the past!* - she could not be wrong now. Because during the Era Armearan, there'd been many a word, which could be taken to mean

54

an array of things depending upon the context, and who'd spoken to whom, and so it went with the word 'heragistra', also.

Unable to prevent herself, she stared pensively at the Prisoner. *'Mistress of Affairs' or 'Lady-in-Command', the two could be one and the same in Armearan - to the extent where, if circumstances and familiarity allowed, the Lady-in-Command title would oft as not be shortened to a simple, 'My Lady'. Why did this feel important?*

She verily burned to ask the prisoner for answers, but yet she didn't move. *A 'My Lady', was not only a respectful bow to a woman of standing and name - during strife it was also an honourable recognition of a martial arts rank and title.*

"So have you had your fill yet, old man?" Simaro spoke up, immediately shattering the artificial notion that the question was anything but rhetorical. "Make your peace with the world and your 'lady' now, My Lord. I am bemused by your behaviour but I have things to attend, so let's get going."

"Lord Simaro, always you ruin." Angemar sighed, a glimmer of sadness stabbing the air between them, as his eyes searched her face for a blink longer. He was still looking for her to recognise him, she realised, but...

But what am I supposed to think, or do, or say? Solancei shook her head, eyes gliding off Angemar.

Retreating a step, she said, "Lord Simaro is right. Let's get this over with."

A New Deal

Simaro stepped forward, more than ready to oblige the blade-whore, but Angemar Cillario was somehow faster.

With a determination only few would have managed with the poisons leaving his body, he shifted, belaying the woman with a gesture that might have soothed a feral dog as he grated, "Mistress of the Light; My Lady? Please wait!"

Cheska from New Wood jolted to a stop. Simaro was on the cusp of damning Angemar's persistence to suit his task, but something told him to abide patience and observe whatever this was just a moment longer.

The prisoner's addled mind would not be stilled on this illusion that he was familiar with this woman, however, Cheska's reactions were intriguing and in the light of her keen offer, perhaps something to ponder the origins of. For sure, something about Cillario's presence; about his condition, had her both at odds and on the defensive, but why? Simaro hadn't dreamt that she would have given herself like this, but with everything left unsaid, she revealed aspects of her own person that hardened his resolve. Angemar was troublesome, but for the future, Simaro would bear the nuisance for a few blinks longer. *For his future and for the prize and recompense owed!*

Though the guards had danced steps to match Angemar as he limped forward, Simaro intercepted their advance with a curt wave, the throbbing of a bruised nose and chin, and the sting of a cut lip, not enough to damage his zeal. *Cillario had spent himself on that stupid stunt, had caught them all off guard, and it had been flecking stupid too - but it would not happen again. The course was set and the signs of Angemar's withdrawal too potent to consider the man capable of a second rally, besides.*

Lazard - the man with a red mark across his throat from where he got punched - frowned sourly at the gesture to hang back, but he always did and Simaro ignored the guard in favour of the two corralled convicts.

"Lord Cillario?" The woman looked puzzled as she made the name both a question and a plead for understanding, "Please, I think we should not waste time on this - your condition..."

"Nah, Mistress, 'tis nothing." Angemar grimaced, a shiver trailing down his body. Based upon Simaro's prior experience and on the way Cillario exhaled each breath on a wheeze, the man was now clearly in pain, and the woman's grey eyes narrowed in concern, flashing to Simaro. *Do something...*

He shrugged, noticing a frigid loathing return to her gaze, then thawing. With a moue of noble disdain for the procrastination, she withdrew her eyes, concentrating on Angemar once more.

"Then, dear Sir, what are we doing here?" she enquired, voice peppered by subtle concern.

"Mistress,-" Angemar started anew, somehow managing to seem less wretched as he paused before her within arm's reach, "-am I mistaken, perhaps? If so I apologise. I... I see that you do not yet speak the old language and if it saddens, it... it cannot be helped. See, there are things, I would speak to you; things that this Venzoian snake cannot know of, but... but this much I can tell you, Mistress: you do not have to endure this for long."

"No indeed-," Simaro felt inspired to inject with a burst of humour and derision, whilst trying to ignore the tender bone of his shoulder blade that had taken the brunt of the impact when Angemar struck,

"-but you keep prolonging your own suffering, don't you! Oh Cillario, you do have some lose chinks in your head!"

Angemar growled like a dog under his breath, a harsh sound of fear and warning; his loathing seemed to rise in the air and forgetting the shoulder, Simaro's smile widened - something to savour he supposed, because for all the loony behaviour and wasted hours, at least he had this now.

As though she'd somehow synchronised her feelings to Angemar's, Cheska's wide mouth distorted to convey her thoughts as well as any spoken words, and for a blink, they both shared an aura of danger - something that warned Simaro that even if Angemar was finished, the grey-eyed twirl was not. *If Angemar had not been sick...*

Simaro twisted from her unwarranted judgement with a smirk to hide a subtle strike of unease. She had no right to her next breath, let along this, however, if the scene played in his favour as imagined, there would not be much she wouldn't do for him, including smiles and the praising of his name to the top of Oriana's peak and back.

"Mistress, don't."

Simaro glared back at the two prisoners, surprise momentarily coursing through his core to see Angemar's fingertips resting lightly on the woman's chest as though he was urging her to stay back.

Seemingly not really aware of the other prisoner, her gaze dead as she beheld Simaro, the woman's eyes seemed to catch and reflect with a silvery lustre in the low red-golden illumination surrounding them.

For a baited heartbeat, Simaro read the coiled violence in her stance. It sent a shiver of supernatural danger across his back, tightening his shoulders: the illusion of something hidden and coveted, causing him to stiffen in preparation for another fight.

"My Lady, please..." Angemar spoke again, and the woman seemed to come to in a rush of unease then, the glazed look in her eyes evaporating like mist to reveal a glimmer of horror instead.

To cover for the strange feeling rising from that just witnessed, Simaro righted himself, slowly relaxing, then grew a wide confident smile into place to demonstrate superior confidence still his. Angemar in return nodded slightly as though pleased and withdrew his touch.

"Oh very well, grey-eyes," Simaro relented, forcing dinted pleasure to ride into the smile; into his stance. "So shall we set the delinquent free?"

"Yes." Cheska licked her lips: a rapid, distracting shift of her features offering brief understanding that she felt disconcerted. Then she seemed to gain a measure of her former calm, for she narrowly continued, "Yes... yes, let him leave! Lord Angemar?"

She regarded Cillario in wide-eyed demand, clearly expecting him to move, but the loon appeared stunned, trapped by a twin set of tremors slowly sideling down his body like a nervous quiver.

"Perhaps he seeks a moment for you to bid him farewell, grey-eyes?"

The woman's eyes sped to Simaro - he presumed to ensure that he wasn't laughing at her nativity or some such.

With a whimsical grimace, he shook off her grounds for concern. "Don't waste it. I am very genuine here, Cheska grey-eyes."

Genuine? The woman seemed to mock the possibility with a subtle expression that might have belonged on a person experiencing a constricting feeling in the chest, but as their eyes met like old adversaries across the negotiating table, she seemed to relent. *There was no trust here of course, but still...*

"I cannot yet go." Angemar straightened imperceptibly as though indignant and gave Simaro a dark look to match a suddenly chilling smile that proved him well and truly stricken by the effects of his 'condition'.

"And you will tell us why?

"Oh, I will tell you snake spawn, so that My Lady will know your true nature."

Simaro snorted, "Oh Angemar you fool, I think she already knows my nature pretty well."

"And she understands too that the idea of my 'freedom' is little but smoke and mirrors to begin with? Is that so? Otherwise one might even name you an oathbreaker, and you know who hunts the oath breakers, don't you?"

Simaro felt his smile pull tight. With effort, he relaxed the muscles in his face to feint indifference, but for a beat, the comment raised the ghosts of obscure stories from a long-lost childhood. Obscenely it left him nonplussed that even now, Cillario should be able to halt him on a whim. He shrugged nonchalantly. "Tales and make-belief to scare the kids of our ancestors? You think to frighten me with old myths and legends that nobody has read about since before the Chaos War? Angemar, Angemar..."

"But I would make a new deal," Angemar injected, one palm absentmindedly clasping the fetter on his left wrist to twist it minutely as if to settle an itch. Successfully ignoring a short tremor, he pulled his spine a little straighter, squaring his shoulders a little more. With a quiver, he stated, "I would make you a new deal: one that cannot be evaded with severed words, unspoken meanings, or double-edged truths; were I you I would take it."

It was sad. Simaro tutted. *Actually tutted.* "Angemar you are too droll-"

"Let my Mistress go!" Angemar's words cut across Simaro's, sharp as a scythe through sheaf. "You don't need her for anything and if you keep her, you will regret it. The Vengeance of Magic stalks her presence wherever she goes and here you are, aligning yourself with Chaos! So you must choose now. *Choose now and choose well!* You cannot win this!"

Half-turning, black eyes glittering, Angemar encompassed Cheska with a look to halt a striking viper. "Now you must take heed Mistress! Take heed, I tell you! Never trust this snake-eyed deceiver! Never! He is in league with Chaos! You understand? Chaos!"

The woman nodded 'yes', but Simaro felt her puzzlement, just as he felt his own bubbling up like gas in a bog. *She didn't understand either; more drivel and make-belief to soothe a broken mind then...?*

Simaro began to laugh. He could not hold back the simple urge and it felt good to sever the man's gifted twaddle. *Never again would he have to listen to this. Never!*

"Ah Cillario, quit rambling would you." Collecting himself a little, Simaro spoke with a genuine smile still backing his words. "I suggest you take this woman's gift and quit trying to bargain for what will never be yours. The mercy of your behaviour surprises me as well, for I assumed that was not the Kerikonese way."

"Perhaps," Angemar heaved a sigh, suppressing a shudder, "But yours is not the Zanzierian way either and my word stands. Let her go. Were you to agree and oblige, I can reassure you it would please you later."

"What would please me, Angemar, would be to see the back of you." Simaro shrugged and hooked both thumbs behind the top of his sword belt to assume a relaxed posture. "Strike his chains."

The soldiers paused. Simaro might have found that funny also, but not now. Not today. Not here.

"Strike his chains." Cheska grey-eyes repeated with a pointed look to match her demand before he could bark at the hapless imbeciles. "Strike them now and let him go."

"Milady, but of course." Simaro agreed with a glib smile and threw a lordly gesture towards the men to oblige.

The two men who'd originally brought Angemar to this little gathering, finally shifted then, one producing a ream of keys and set about finding the right stub to fit the round locks of the wrist irons. It was a noisy but relatively simple process. Soon a rattle of lose chain pronounced the job done and Cheska stared as the older prisoner slipped from the D-shaped manacles the moment they sprang open, the heavy links slithering like a heavy snake over the edge of a branch to form a small harmless heap at Angemar's feet.

Ignoring the subtle shivers that quivered across his body, the other man rubbed the tender skin of his wrists, suddenly pinning Simaro with a hard stare.

Seemed the loon was determined to be foolish. Shame...

Signalling one of his men to step forth, and with a nod towards the woman, Simaro warned Angemar, "Try your worst now and she will die by your actions! Your turn to choose wisely now!"

In speaking the words, steel whistled a soft tune and out of nowhere the now hard-eyed man that Cheska grey-eyes had tried to strangle in the corridor - *Simaro forgot his name* - slanted the grey blade of his sword under her chin.

He noted she barely seemed upset, even when she had little choice to back away as directed. *Just a small insurance against mishaps.* He was certain she understood this as well: Angemar certainly did as he fell quiet, his body releasing something that might have been interpreted as scavenged energy.

"You wish for this to go the way you have begged me on so many occasions, you do not raise your hand against me and mine again or there will no longer be a bargain, do you hear?"

Angemar's face was bland. An unreadable mask to compliment toneless words. "I hear you liar. I hear you."

"So be on your way then," Simaro urged Angemar, "Go now - or would you keep the lady in suspense, old man?"

Angemar stopped rubbing his wrist and offered Simaro a very lucid look; a look so full of disgust and unspoken hate, that Simaro momentarily feared he'd completely misjudged what the mad Kerikonese would still be capable of, but as a new tremor rattled his frame, lasting longer than the previous attacks, that witnessed anger faltered, pain pulling it apart in a lour that couldn't lie.

"Set My Lady free," Angemar pressed out through clenched teeth, "Set her free."

Simaro hissed a sigh, invariably drawing short-tempered. "My mad friend, let's make a new bargain then if you would: you are free to go and I am letting you take the bitch along if you must see her free too, but be on your way! You will know what to do, I feel."

Having chosen his words with care, Simaro stepped a little to one side, dismissing Angemar with a prissy wave as though done with

63

his company. Of course, the mad prisoner hesitated. *Who would not?* The New Wood twirl on the other hand...

With her eyes travelling from Angemar to the soldiers still stationed in the slight semi-circle of attention they'd assumed upon him releasing the prisoner, Simaro knew she'd be speculating not only if she might truly be able to trust her imminent release, just as she'd be wondering if the men would indeed move - because currently, Angemar would have to shoulder his way past.

Angemar shivered and the woman frowned, dark brows dropping to give her a forbidding brooding look. He could read that she feared something was definitely not right, but she didn't understand what. *Surprises did not commonly appeal to him, but perhaps on this occasion...?*

Her eyes flickered to Angemar. He had not moved.

"My Lord Angemar?" Searching for guidance, the cadence of her voice remained even but the alluring dark lilt was back.

"You are indeed such a double-faced rat." Ignoring her, a harsh smiled bent Angemar's lips as he looked at Simaro but his voice came low and noble, loaded with contempt. "Your terms are too steep. I will run the gauntlet for your amusement; I will attempt the impossible to further your point! If you consent, I will perform the show you wish of me, but I would have your word on pain of death that she will be free and unharmed, or else the Hunters will have you!"

"Cillario, is the idea of freedom really so abhorrent that you must question my intentions?" Simaro goaded.

"Freedom, no! Your interpretation, yes! And if you wish for me to do this now, I will, but not with her! I demand that you set her free!"

The man was relentless. It was pointless.

64

Solancei drew a breath. "Please, Lord Angemar. If we can go, let's go!"

Still ignoring her, Angemar's voice rose louder, some of his former authority coming to life,   "Release my Mistress now and I will 'leave' as you 'suggest', otherwise toss me to the flames below for I will not make this so easy for you!"

The woman sighed in frustration and confusion, and no wonder. Simaro sighed too; a huff really, which clearly showed his fading patience. This was taking much longer and required far more efforts than he'd imagined necessary and rather that soothing his already ruffled temper to have the twirl go gallivanting on her own through the old dungeon, he felt the return of his former, short temper.

Without another word, Simaro closed the gap between the two of them with a few brisk paces. Then, pushing the guard aside, he propelled her forward with a firm tug that made her stumble to right herself or else trip over her own legs.

"You want a new deal, here it is! You are so concerned for your 'Mistress'? I told you: here she is! It's what I'll give you. Take her now! But if you are sure you want to make this bargain, you know it involves a choice for you, madman. You see, either she leaves with you. Through those tunnels there-" Simaro pointed across the chasm to the dark fissures behind the Demonai, "-or, she stays here. With me! For just a little while longer. I promise you she will live: for old time sake, I will make this pledge. Now what say you?"

For a moment Angemar couldn't hide shock. "You know I cannot."

"Oh, but why?" Simaro basked in the knowledge that Angemar was cornered. Across the chasm, the Demonai appeared to be perking up at the change they undoubtedly sensed in the air and chains rattled as the biggest one shifted with just the smallest of growls.

With a wink towards the woman, he pushed, "Is it your choice, Cillario? Would you not even ask her?"

Angemar exhaled like a defeated man, a quiver taking the strength just a little from his posture.

"Mistress," he began forlornly, as though embarrassed, "I will-"

"It's not necessary; really!" Eyes on the Demonai, the woman interrupted, "We... we can..."

"Think about it now. Strategically." Simaro encouraged, knowing the task inhuman and the challenge cruel, yet not caring. *He needed her here...*

Her eyes glazed over again, but for a blink, he could feel her do the calculations. Even if Angemar did not show any fear at the sight of the Hyatts, could she muster similar? He suspected that the mere thought of going anywhere near the abominations petrified her - Angemar was still hurt; could not even stand entirely straight; they had no armour; no protection, no weapons - unless they did not mind arriving minus a couple of body parts, how could they possibly both escape?

"One of us might distract the Demonai," she began haltingly, her tone betraying the truth, "One of us might make it past relatively unscathed, and..."

Angemar trembled. "My Lady, I am not willing to give such madness thought."

Cheska shivered, averting her gaze in desperate thought. "No, but..."

"My Lady, don't trouble yourself," Angemar gave her a piercing, weary look that would have suited a soldier on a battlefield about to join the last volley against an overwhelming enemy force.

She opened her mouth to speak, but Angemar went to her, clasping her hands in his and Simaro saw her startle as her eyes caught sight of the man's odd body paint that had encircled his wrists and forearms ever since Simaro had first laid eye on him. She might not have noticed earlier. In the poor light they did not stand out against the grime and healed cuts, but as the prisoner gently raised her hands to his lips, the torn sleeves revealed the strange intertwining symbols drawn in multiple colours of ink and something might appear to be gold-dust inlaid beneath the skin. Angemar had only told him the tattoos were tribal, nothing more; Simaro had wondered why a man would deface his own body like that and had amused himself defiling the patterns on and off with instruments of varying fancy, yet as the skin seemed to heal, the ink eventually settling back over the surface as though by magic, he'd lost interest in the small game. Of course, he knew one Tuxaman loon who would have relished the chance to examine the limbs but he did not have time to oblige and ice for the packing would be expensive; Keriko folk were not known to subject themselves to tattoos, but where there were one, there'd be another. *For now, the Tuxaman had enough curiosities...*

"You go then. I made this choice already," the woman stated, raising her eyes from the inked pictures to peer at Angemar's face.

A profanity escaped Angemar but the remainder of his spirits seemed to leave him then. The woman, in turn, looked on with earnest pity.

67

"Why does he think he knows me?" she enquired suddenly, still looking at Angemar, unable or perhaps unwilling to contain her questions any longer. "What has made him so… delusional? What have you done to him?"

A flare of excitement sifted through Simaro. The question was perfect. She was about to crawl like a puppy to the sound of his voice!

"Ah grey-eyes, hate to let you down but this is not all to my credit, I fear." Simaro felt regret to admit the truth, but amidst it all, the exhilaration overpowered the facts of the past. "Yes, sadly I can assure you that he was already quite mad when he first arrived here: raving about this Alérathnar person, about keys and locks and this *something* called… what was it? Oh yes… this… this vengeance of magic, as you've heard."

Recounting each point with bored sarcasm, Simaro fleetingly gave the impression that he was beyond care, yet he continued, the rise in emotional investment prompting him to speak just a tad faster than ideal, "Gods, and we've heard it all so many times now too - although, I must tell you that the 'Mistress part' is wholly new! Gods' death, the crazed man has not seen a woman in over three seasons so who am I to judge? Perhaps he just likes you?"

A hard bark of mirth escaped the woman, "My… now I seriously doubt that!"

"Well perhaps, grey-eyes. All that said, however, the Meer'ron did nothing to improve his unstable imagination." Simaro sucked down a breath to still the canter within, cast her a quick glance and elaborated, "In fact, I don't mind telling you that we thought he was sent to spy; I thought that perhaps he was fainting madness as a ruse to avoid the questioning, so we had to find out, and he fled the

68

city. Guess when we finally caught up and put him to question, our methods may have unhinged him."

The woman's nostrils flared and if not for Angemar still clasping her hands she might have backed away.

"You know of Meer'ron?" he asked innocently and watched her face turn chalky. Continuing lightly, he remarked, "Poisons are of course never pleasant, but I have been told by some out-of-business Hedge Wizard that the State of Veranto and Meer'ron do not go well together. It seems… hmm, it seems to have some undesirable side effects - at least, so I'm told, though right now this is undoubtedly not of any interest, so let's concentrate on our dear Lord Angemar."

For a moment silence ruled.

"You deliberately poisoned him?" Simaro could see the pulse point in the woman's throat as it fluttered like a trapped insect against her skin. "You… you deliberately stole the man's physical - and mental - health?!"

"Not deliberately, no - more out of necessity." Simaro smiled pleasantly as a string of quivers muddled through Angemar as if to showcase his condition. The woman gaped at the man's trembling hands around hers and looked repulsed, but then her face turned serene. *The blessings of Veranto?*

"So was he?" Her grey-eyes swivelled to his, making him lament for a moment that he would not see them in daylight for some time. "A spy I mean?"

Simaro pinned his stare to hers for a breath too long, then shook himself. "What? Oh no, far from it grey-eyes. The draughts of Meer'ron revealed him nothing more sinister than a member of some obscure cult that no one has ever even heard of, but he had connections; was in possessions of some intriguing items. Still, one might say that he was simply unfortunate enough to find himself in the wrong place at the wrong time, but is that not how it always goes?"

The woman looked set to argue, then her features smoothed, but her colour had not recovered. He said, "Today is the day I no longer need Lord Angemar, though - so here we are."

She paled a little more. He was pleased she got the reference. *Gods, the temples always picked the bright ones...*

"Now if it pleases, I beg of you just one thing before this goes the way it must?" Angemar appeared to draw her back from some imaginary cliff, because she gathered herself, the mask of serenity flowing smoothly into place once more as she honoured his attention.

Angemar smiled like a father looking upon his only daughter on the day of her mother's funeral. "Please Mistress, if you would? Please remember my name till we see each other again and in the meantime think of me well. Do not upset yourself over this: it cannot be changed. It just cannot."

For a moment Angemar's words hypnotised Simaro and the woman looked equally shocked. It was with good reason, he thought. *Angemar's words might be intelligible but he could not possibly think she'd seek him out when this was all done, could he? Why was he trying to fill her with pretty lies and make-beliefs? Angemar knew what this was. Even if the twirl did not - Angemar knew!*

Cheska shook her head 'yes'. A quiver sailed through Angemar and Simaro saw the woman's doubt then. *She was humouring him...*

"Then be easy now, My Lady." Ignoring the truth, or – more likely – simply oblivious in his condition, Angemar soothed the woman with a tender smile that almost softened the emaciated planes of his sharp features in a way that reminded Simaro how the man had looked upon the day they'd first met. It was yet to be seen if it had been worth their time listening to the loon's mad ramblings and half-cut deranged imaginings, but Simaro guessed the proof would be linked to the Tuxaman's success. It was not yet time for that revelation - but as for this... here and now...

"Please?" the woman pleaded with the older man again, her voice drying up, as she cast around for words, yet shook her head in defeat. *It was an odd sight.* Angemar was near-tall as Simaro himself; when they'd met he'd been on the stocky side too, but now his once-broad frame was as bent as an old serf who'd worked every one of his fifty summers toiling behind a plough in the fields beyond Zanzier and the woman had barely to tilt her head to look him in the eye. Angemar had resisted and fought his own demise since the very first day, but now it was finally over: no matter what the woman from New Wood imagined, no matter what Cillario said to bolster faith, it was over...

With a last lingering look, Kerikonese renegade surrendered her hands and stepped back.

"Now till we meet again Mistress: may your heart sing with courage, your mind with conviction, and your body with health." Angemar trembled hard and drew a haggard breath. "You must have faith that this will be well: trust that I will be waiting by the edge of the forest to greet you and that borrowed sword of yours, and please... if I do not know you, then I swear... Mistress, go easy on me, would you? Kaisor Steel cuts friend or foe or Venzoian equally deep

71

and I will always be amongst the ones you and yours call friends. Remember that, My Lady. Remember - and beware for the sake of what you love!"

Again the woman nodded, too stunned it seemed by the words coming out of Angemar, but Simaro was not far behind. *Had the poison really taken the man's mind that deep then? Angemar knew what must happen and he prattled on. On and on! Gods, if someone was to lend the New Wood twirl a Kaisor blade it would be a stunning gift of trust and generosity! But who'd be stupid enough?*

Watching the weird exchange, Simaro could verily see the woman thinking the exact same. *And forest? What forest? And what the fleck was this 'whensoian', he suddenly kept referring to as if it were a curse?*

Simaro sucked in a long deep breath, clearing his mind. The illusions were in Angemar's head, and perhaps not something to be rejected though Simaro was rarely that compassionate. But the more Kerikonese man spoke, the better the effect on the woman. Gods, the place was roasting, and his shoulder was telling him a tale of discomforts to come, but good! It was all flecking worth it!

"My Lord, I don't think we will be-"

"Mistress, you must listen now. And listen well!" Angemar scattered her brittle words, unexpectedly clasping both her shoulders as if to input gravity, though a shudder ruffled across his frame. "So bastard snake-eyes wins! For now! And so, you must stay! And learn! My Lady, whatever happens, you must remain steadfast! This couple of lowbred, mindless Rippers our poisonous traitor has forced on leashes cannot have you, but don't look away now! Learn! You must prevail, do you understand? You must!"

"But you-"

"Here our paths must separate," Angemar gave her a tight smile as if to apologise for interrupting, "but I can offer you a little advice: though life has a way of twisting everything away from us, it also gives us back the most unbelievable gifts. I am sorry that I cannot make your journey easier - I would've liked to have stood with you to the end but this will have to be enough, I see this and I am content."

Angemar wet his lips, seemingly fighting some inner battle. "Apologies, a little more hope for you to clutch in the darkest of hours would perhaps have been kind, but alas since you do not recall the old language as I thought, I cannot tell you too much. Simply know that you will get through this! The future of the Nine Realms depends on you! When asked to step up, do not deny!"

The Nine Realms? Step up...?

"Angemar! This is done!" Simaro sang at him, the lilting reminder both a warning and a nudge.

Angemar hissed like a feral cat even though his dark eyes didn't waver. "Remember: you will know freedom again Mistress! Just not as soon as I."

"Freedom?" she protested. Gesturing to convey sharp cynicism, she slung a hand towards the other ledge. Her voice climbed an octave, "You mean to do ask he asks then? But... but that is not freedom! I don't mean to question you fighting skills, but-"

"Shush!" Angemar demanded, staring at her one blink longer. With a shudder, he whispered, "Gods hate, you are so young, Mistress, but I am thankful to have laid eyes on you again. Feel no sorrow! My Lady, this is only the beginning of your journey. And we will meet again."

"Angemar! Now! Or she goes with you!" Simaro snapped and the man shivered, though it appeared, sadly not from the attention of the harsh warning words.

"Do not be tempted by useless flattery," Angemar injected rapidly as though he knew himself unable to stall further, "Many will try to use you, others will want to possess you; abominations will try to bend you to their course. But remember my words: only one is truly worthy of you! Only one will fight for you! Only one will risk eternity to win you back! Do you understand?"

Solancei shook her head, and Angemar stood back. "Alérathnar embrace me - now I can pass on with hope for the future and that is good!"

"But-"

Like a bear faced by a hunter, Angemar snarled in her face. Shifting, a new light of madness seemed to smother the place where sentient rationality and thought had briefly ruled and with an unexpectedly sharp push he repelled her from his vicinity, the unexpected rejection sending her stumbling backwards.

Eyes riveted to Angemar in denial of the rejection, she was panting hard in shock and suppressed a whimpered as Simaro caught her and kept her from falling squarely onto her backside. She righted herself with a twist - like a cat pushed from a tree to land on its feet - and shot clear of him.

Simaro let her be with a smirk of tiny triumph. The emotion was draining from her eyes, fading as though she was protecting something deep within and Simaro knew that kind of look; had seen it before. *She was bleeding metaphorically speaking: hurt by the man's betrayal no doubt, and surely fearing every single word spoken about Meer'ron after this...*

74

Utterly oblivious of the woman he'd just been prepared to honour with titles and protection, Angemar now fixated his dark stare entirely onto Simaro - his focus re-animated only for this purpose it seemed.

"Now tell me, Friend of Chaos,-" he whispered, "-if I am to be made a spectacle of this hour, do I at least get a weapon to make it interesting?!"

Running the Gauntlet

Solancei felt surrounded by traps and enemies, her mind hopelessly trying to keep up and adjust, but she couldn't. *If an elaborate plot to drive her insane, Simaro was winning; perhaps he'd already had won. When he'd mentioned Meer'ron...!*

She quenched a shiver of fear. *As if her head was far away she heard Simaro respond to Angemar's irony-laced 'request...* "If a weapon you desire, then a weapon you shall have. Lieutenant, give the man the seax."

The soldier with the neat beard obeyed with a curt nod, his eyes momentarily flickering as he removed the bull knife he'd retrieved from her earlier and threw it at Angemar's feet. It landed with a loud clatter that jarred her senses, but Angemar did not seem touched, nor did he instantly bend to pick it up. Despite the mad gleam in his eye, he gathered some hidden seed of will to straighten up tall and Solancei could only imagine what effort it might cost him to pretend that he had not just been beaten or was finding himself wracked by the effects of Meer'ron poison.

"Inmoriatu Wan Talari an Benuriatu Estivivar, Heragistra!" he intoned with an unhinged look in her direction. *"We of the Alérathnar's Brotherhood say: live well and die another day!"*

The Veranto Link soaring and detracting, she nodded. The strange words meant nothing to her, and yet she was held captive as Angemar's attention continued to burn like hot augers against her; then she almost spooked when he suddenly pounced forward, dipping like a striking falcon to scoop up the forlorn seax with one hand to flip it around in his palm as though ready to pursue conflict. It had the men nearly scrambling to intercept all over; had Simaro

76

fumble for his bastard-sized rapier as he retreated a step with a curt oath under his breath, but the prisoner did not act as imagined.

"The Brotherhood of Alérathnar prevail!" he shouted with an edge of triumph, turning so smoothly on his heel that his injuries seemed a thing-imagined when he sprang directly towards the chasm, barely pausing at the edge before launching himself off over the drop.

It made Solancei screech in wordless denial until she saw the top of his head pop up over the rim just a little further to the left. *He'd landed on the ledge,* she realised, heart still fluttering, and not sure whether to cheer or cry.

"He has the fogs of Osari'Chi rolling round his head. He is utterly mad," she heard the soldier directly to her left whisper with a lilt of disbelief.

Another responded with a snort of mirth, "Certainly, he does! Well either that, or else he be possessed by the lure of Arbar'Chi. Some sods just want to die… there is no reason."

"Maybe the Gods have promised him three Kheltian whores for company whilst he walks the Void?" a third man commented, "Who could resist then?"

All three men laughed, but the sound got swallowed. The Demonai had come to life as Angemar proceeded to race along the precarious path and Solancei wanted to clap her hands over her ears as they began to roar with menacing challenge. She had no inkling what Angemar might be feeling right then; there was simply no telling as he gradually disappeared beneath the lip of rock, the hewn-out ledge somehow leading him on a trajectory out of sight from their position. From the reactions of the abominations, she could gauge his progress easily though; the creatures were straining their chains, spinning their bodies towards the narrow shelf in the darkest corner where their ledge seemed to begin. If their reactions thus far were anything to go by, she expected they'd go buck-wheat, kicking-colt crazy the moment Angemar reached their domain.

The ice in her core burned, pulled, yet though distracting, she couldn't look away. Angemar appeared sooner than she'd hoped. Looping from a space of shadows and air, leaping like an acrobat with the hounds of Osari'Chi snapping at his heels to ford a section of missing stone before finally arriving on wider footing directly on the far side of the chasm.

As though halted by an invisible force, there he paused and crouched, and for a moment the sooty-red creatures seemed turned to solid stone as they too stilled completely to observe their would-be prey with a ferocious aura rising from their emaciated muscle and ugly faces. As though lit by tiny lanterns from within, the gleam of yellow-green eyes held the near-palpable feral longing for blood, but it was the consistent tune of the low-pitched growls that would certainly cause her marrow to jellify if continued.

Distressingly, there was something quite human about their deliberate conduct as they mirrored Angemar who likewise hadn't moved a muscle. *Was that intelligence she was witnessing? Or simple animalistic behaviour? And did it matter?*

For now, Angemar would be safe unless he stepped forward; from where he'd paused, she judged him privy to a ten-to-twelve pace safety-zone before contact - enough for now, but...

Would Angemar do it? She had no idea. *Every eye was on the absurd spectacle but the man himself seemed oblivious to all but the two abominations. Where was the exit? Was he trying to formulate an angle of attack? Was he mentally adjusting - or just hovering out of fear, and exhaustion, and Meer'ron damage?*

Solancei knew that had she been forced to go there too, she couldn't have moved past another two paces. It just wouldn't have happened, but Angemar was different through and through. *Perhaps...*

Oddly she recalled his hands upon hers: the warmth of another human's touch, bizarrely comforting to her for a change, although his skin had felt dry and cracked: the palms callused from the sword and the fingertips careworn like a bard's; like someone used to playing the Kithara. *What would Angemar do? He could not just stand there, but nor could he return.*

Solancei tried to penetrate the air and blanketing atmosphere to study the deep, wider fissures in the rock between the Demonai - and perhaps she caught the notion of a break in the wall after all: something slightly paler than the surrounding darkness?

Was this where Angemar needed to go? Would he need to aim for that route? Straight past the two hungry creatures? She chewed her bottom lip, fear on his behalf curling like an attentive cat in and around her limbs.

Slowly, very slowly, the prisoner began to rise, his every move meticulously careful and strangely unobtrusive.

Solancei wanted him to stop. One of the Demonai growled, a deep vibration in the air, and she felt the man to her right shiver as he mumbled, "Mercy..."

Mercy, yes... but not bloody likely! Biting her lip, she forgot about her own plight, forgot about everything else whilst Angemar uncurled like a flower to the sun of the Demonai's presence.

An echo of his parting words provoked drifting icicles down her spine as she watched. *Inmoriatu Wan Talari an Benuriatu Estivivar.* Everything about him was a question. She couldn't remember, but there was something familiar about the High Armearan words after all: something seen or read somewhere, but she couldn't think...

Solancei's gut clenched with the sensation of the shadowy unknown as the words spun in time to the Demonai chorus. She didn't think her heart could slam against her ribs any faster and yet the beat seemed to intensify: the mad prisoner had started sideling towards the Hyatts - calmly, deliberate, each move seemed sleek as humanly possible - but the seax barely more than an afterthought, if she were to trust the angle of the blade.

One more step... and another... The Demonai seemed to watch him in suspense, but in five paces and he'd be upon them - or they on him! *Live well and die another day? He couldn't be serious, could he?* As he got closer to them, Solancei made the staggering realisation that the two Hyatts were taller than she'd first gauged – Angemar's presence gave her something by which to reference their true size and stature - and it seemed neigh-on impossible that he should be able to win through.

Silently, she cursed Simaro a good few times. Of course, this was not what she'd intended when she'd pleaded for Angemar's release, but the understanding that he had been made a Meer'ron addict by Simaro's hand, had undeniably served to quench her fight to maintain an opinion of what was right or not. *Still, for this mad venture alone, the Gods ought to reward him - yet she feared that his endeavour to gain freedom in this manner - whilst without a doubt brave - would also be nothing short of suicidal!*

Gods, but she did not want to see his demise, though. Selfishly, she craved answers: he'd thrown her random pearls of words that almost meant something - *or so she'd thought* - but now she wasn't so sure. Was he was going to get himself killed before she'd get a chance to find out!

Front teeth warring at her lower lip and fearing what would be, Solancei stood riveted, but amazingly, Angemar's subtle approach seemed to have confused the creatures.

He appeared without fear too. *So maybe he could do it? If the monsters were slowed by hunger...?*

She swallowed hard, tasting the lingering oppression of her own terror like a sticky tit-bit in her mouth: cloying and sweet, acerbic and thick. *Angemar, for the love of whatever you hold dear, do this! Do this and win free and I will come and find you,* she pledged, conjuring a glimmer of faith. *Perhaps... perhaps if he was fast enough? Perhaps...?*

It was a fool's naive twist to hold a speck of illusion though. Within her, the Veranto seemed to grow huge like a monster in its own right, filling her with a strange sense of acceptance that she had wasted hope on the idea that she could have made any difference to the older prisoner. Aggressive approach or not, the two creatures were not blind to the cautious man and their blackened claws were curling as though in preparation...

Solancei felt the frozen splinters of fractured icicles rip down her spine, making her body seem too narrow to hold both the Veranto and the ice, but she did not have room to care. If he wanted to reach that fissure in the wall, he'd have to get closer. Much closer.

'Don't look away,' he'd bid her - and Gods forgive her, even had she wanted to, she couldn't! Morbidly fascinated and repulsed all at the same time, she couldn't even blink. *Maybe if he ran, ducked and flung himself into a forward roll; maybe...*

81

Staring straight at the Demonai, Angemar hefted the Seax as if to test the weapon's balance. "Gods beyond, let it be quick!" she muttered to herself, only for Angemar to make her heart leap when he proceeded to do something very much unexpected. A seax was not of a design which lent itself to throwing, yet Angemar did just that.

Raising the knife in one fluid transition of power, he launched the long blade with barely a beat's pause for adjustment to the way it must perform given the fact that most the weight sat centred within the three inches of the spine closest to the handle and was countered more in the edge near the tip than at the rear bolster-

Solancei knew she stilled on a heartbeat, holding her breath. The bold action also earned him oaths of surprise from the men behind her as the ungainly seax flew, handle over blade - not to down or debilitate any of the Hyatts but to embed itself in something wooden with a resounding twang. Disturbed, the Demonai swivelled as if surprised - roar momentarily directed at the point behind them where the seax had disappeared in shadows and shifting streamers of fledgling light.

It made no odds.

Angemar had missed! As it must, a wave of consternation hit her. *She'd seen the weapon fly past the creatures with good space to spare for margins if one were to split hairs. Neither Hyatt had been hit, nor even grazed - the uncannily loud noise as the blade connected elsewhere could not leave room for hope or false interpretation.*

'Hopeless fool, this is it." Behind her to the left, one of the soldiers giggled under his breath. "I hope they take his legs first."

"Lazard, speak of fools!" another accused, a deliberate whiny edge of provocation to his lowered voice, "They never take the legs first! Five bronze Marks that it'll be his face? Like a melon - pop!"

"Drang, I say the legs and I will take that bet!" the other shot back, shy of a loud whisper just as someone else shushed their morbid sport.

They felt silent but Solancei's stomach was already turning, the ice carving new hollows that the State of Veranto just didn't seem able to ford. *The legs or the head...?!*

And yet for all her terror, Angemar did not seem concerned as he sauntered towards the Demonai, now empty-handed. *Three paces. Just three. Then two...*

Freedom Shall be Mine

One of the creatures growled, the other soon adding its voice to the warning as it coiled in readiness now - but never faltering, Angemar hauled back his ragged sleeves to reveal the full length of the heavy tattoos Solancei had previously spotted.

To her, he looked like someone about to enter a game of fisticuffs but then a strange feeling sailed through her core as she saw him raise both forearms like a vertical shield before his own torso. It was another oddly fluid move, she noted, elegantly executed and for some reason it drew a strange, almost immediate reaction from both Hyatt'Raah - because they fell silent on the same blink, something about their stance altering to lose the ferocious readiness too.

Solancei gasped like she was surfacing a lake after a deep dive, feeling the air race abrasively down her throat: too warm, too dry. First one, then the other, the Hyatts withdrew one sinuous step from Angemar, then another, and another, quite as though compelled by some invisible force to do so.

Openly gaping at the unexpected development, Solancei was a moment in seeing the presence of a soft nimbus - like that of a distant star. She was yet a moment longer in realising that it came not from any lantern, but from the inked forms on Angemar's arms!

In the hushed golden light, the swirling designs looked suddenly vivid and prominent even from afar; it must be the distance and the state of her mind, but for a blink she could have also sworn the handsome symbols were moving like the slithering bodies of a full nest of vipers around his skin: undulating, curling, but as she blinked, she saw yet again only the emanating glow of sheltered light.

It reminded her of the fields of fluorescent fungus that thrived on the vertical slants of Oriana's Mountain back in Etruia. She and Iambre would sometimes linger to observe the phenomenon when they came to colour just after dusk. *Green, and red, and blue... mingling together and blending as though alive, but an illusion nonetheless. Just an illusion...*

Blinking twice, she resisted the urge to rub her eyes. The heat combined with her intense stare was making her eyes water and her vision dance, but again the question of Angemar's goal persisted to overshadow personal discomforts.

Was he simply going to walk past the Demonai? Was that his plan? Solancei shifted as if she was walking at his heels.

As the monsters continued to shrink into submission, their peculiar thin bodies bending to obey this silent pressure Angemar appeared to assert, she was inspired to notions of awe. *What was happening was both flecking impossible and brilliant and she couldn't take her eyes off of the sight.*

The air was pregnant with expectation. On her right, she heard a guard gasp in surprise at what he saw, his subsequent loud intake of breath almost comical but for the fact that she might very well have mirrored his sentiment without realising. Angemar looked indeed as if he was simply hoping to walk straight past the lethal creatures with nothing more to protect him than a pair of dirty arms and upraised hands. *He must have known he could do this, but Gods... How could he be so fearless? He had them in his thrall somehow - creatures and human alike - but could it last?*

At the thought, her core rolled in denial. The glinting eyes of the nightmarish things promised no hope as they watched him with hate, but still they retreated as if to avoid contact with something repulsive just the same. *The prisoner was gliding forward, ever forward: inside the reach of claws and teeth now.*

Solancei felt herself flinch, almost unable to stay still - however, the abominations only bent their necks and bowed away from him, their chains hanging slack as they cowered in his presence, sinking lower, ever lower, till it seemed they might be kneeling.

They cannot attack, she realised, *Kira'Cha's mercy: somehow what he's doing stops them! Mercy...*

She unclenched her fists, unaware that she'd tensed up, clearly from the disbelief that coursed with the notion of crushed ice through her veins. *Gods... this made no sense. That Retzken had wanted to Hunt; to take the first swipe - yet it now bend from the task as if it had lost all aggression. It looked like something out of a tale. It looked like... like magic.*

Staring till she thought her eyes might pop, Solancei watched Angemar venture another step; impossibly the Demonai bowed deeper, and...

He was within deep shadows now. The strange glow that seemed to spring from his tattoos lit up the dark just enough to reveal the seax embedded in a dark metal-studded door. *Freedom! It was possible then...*

She started to smile. Like saturation in the air, it seemed to her that she could feel Angemar's concentration as he went - she did not know how, but she could sense it in her core - and in two steps he'd be free!

Lightheaded now, Solancei felt the soldiers' quiet stupefaction as the Demonai continued to comply. She didn't understand though. What was the prisoner was waiting for? He could have easily reached for the centrally-placed metal handle to push open the door and step from danger - yet instead he paused, then turned to face his odd audience with an unsteady waver that forced him to adjust minutely to stand tall.

To Solancei it was clear that he was he was tired beyond tired. She saw him heave a breath and move his head in a way to reveal that weariness was indeed tugging at his reserves but it didn't matter. Her smile grew a little wider and her eyes flickered to Simaro, enjoying his perplexed expression.

Eat that you flecking maggot! Her thoughts were fierce. *This triumph is worth a stack of ten Gold Plates; no more! What had he said earlier? Something about maze designs? Was this what the sinuous patterns on Angemar's arms really were? Mazes to hold impossible creatures?*

In a flash, the complex mosaic patterns of the tunnels sprang to mind. *It seemed it was too easy, but maybe...?*

For a blink, she wanted to laugh hysterically but found she couldn't press forth a sound. Angemar held her attention. *Why had he stopped? This was all madness! As cuckoo as two alien bloodhounds with claws like mythical daggers and red-scaled hides like fabled dragons looking to tear their way through anything or anyone getting in their path-kind-of-cuckoo! Angemar should run! Why did he linger?* She didn't like that his arms were starting to shake in earnest now. As if from the strain of hard physical labour... *the Demonai bowed lower, crouching, pacified... come on, Angemar!*

Solancei chanced a glance at the men surrounding her. Bemusing to her eye, the entire group looked pole-axed. She was unaware if the other men saw the cost on Angemar, though. *She prayed that he was nearly done; prayed...*

Across the chasm, Angemar executed just one tiny gesture then: a small action that looked as if he simply flexed his hands and flung away something that might have clung to them. Then the picture seemed to solidify and she could see him relax - however still taking great pains in lowering his arms one minuscule fraction at a time: a worrying contrast to the rapid rise and fall his chest and shoulders evident, as he heaved-in gulps of great breaths in line with the assaulting quivers.

"My Lady, behold then!" Angemar's well-mannered voice sounded gravelly with fatigue as he demanded her attention with the lilt of his voice. Assured of her eyes, he wrenched the seax out of the wood, and still amazed at what she was witnessing, Solancei wholly expected him to push through the door then, yet again he refrained.

The lack of action made her blink but neither abomination moved although a low growl kept vibrating from the throat of one on the right: a lingering reminder that all was not entirely casual.

Somewhere near, a man snatched a harsh breath and she was almost amused to realise the sound had come from Simaro himself. *What? Things did not go to plan?* She felt like taunting him, but then Angemar spoke again.

"My Lady," he repeated, louder now, the light from the symbols on his arms painting shadows in the hollows beneath his cheekbones and in the folds of his ragged clothing as they continued to glow, "as I told you before: there are many things that I would have revealed onto you. Many! However that whore's son knows nothing of the world that matters; please extend me your forgiveness, yet I would rather it sat that way for a while longer - so to prevent disaster, you understand?"

Solancei nodded though she doubted if Angemar could have seen in the semi-dark but Simaro grimaced openly.

"I might know nothing," he shouted then with a cavalier attitude that made her flesh crawl, "however, I still know that this is the End of you!"

"The End?" Solancei flung at him, the ice within rising like flecks of crystal that seemed to shade her vision momentarily like a snowstorm hazing everything. Spinning to face him, she let her voice rise a notch. "The End? Are you demented? He is free! Free! Your hags look be-spelled and any blink now, he's going to saunter through that door! You lost!"

"My Lady!" As if he'd heard their exchange clear as bells, Angemar called her attention back to his presence and she halted further onslaught.

Angemar took a moment allowing a quiver to pass, then said, "My Lady, save your words, for his are not false. My journey will end here today, of that we can be certain. You see, the door at my back does not lead anywhere - I know this because the tunnels behind it have collapsed. And indeed, I know of this because it happened when I tried to slay these two Rippers here. This place is cursed! I knew that: it's slowly sinking into the ground! If only I'd come a little sooner... a little earlier..."

She heard the caustic, near-fatalistic calm in his voice - as though it was but ice upon the well in the morning - but the words bound Solancei regardless. Rather than blood, it seemed it was now cold, cold frost that suddenly raced through her veins and her heart skipped a beat as her anger swelled. *Angemar had been aware. Simaro had made him play this game and for that alone the cold creature within deserved... deserved...*

The ice seemed to grow purer: transparent near-enough and through the hundreds of already existing chinks in her hold on Veranto, a sense of righteous indignation forced the fractions to expand till she felt herself creak like old wood from the pressure. *Simaro deserved a fate worse than death for this! He deserved-*

"You filthy son of a rat!" Never one to curb her mouth at the best of times, the curse slipped out before she'd had the chance to consider the consequences but she didn't care when the guards had to wrestle her back from Simaro.

"You knew this would happen!" she hissed, "You knew, and yet you used him to raise hope! May the Gods rain plague on you! You disgust me!"

Spitting at his face in anger, only just missing him, Solancei wrestled against the guards to little avail.

"Oh grey-eyes, don't get so uptight about it all. There is no need, really." Simaro's tone was conciliatory. "You don't know me well but I think you'll come to understand that Angemar knew the truth of deal he'd been dealt. It is all a simple question of interpretation. Soon you might understand his decision too - perhaps even embrace it."

Simaro turned, ostensibly dismissing her wrath, and as if on cue, one of the red creatures growled a heart-stopping warning.

Freedom... The word echoed in her mind. *And she might have known, Gods curse it! High Armearan was not the only language where words might carry different interpretations depending on the situation! Gods curse it!*

Angry though she were, Solancei stilled against the soldiers. She observed a shadow pass through Angemar then: a ripple that travelled the length of his body. It was not much, but it seemed to send a signal to the Demonai, and slowly, ever so slowly, much like they were straining against a set of unseen bonds, both Hyatts began to move, straightening…

"No!" Solancei spat the word like a jilted lover in fear she'd lost everything as she resumed to battle against the hands that detained her.

Eyes whipping from Angemar to Simaro and back, she pleaded. "You can stop this! They will kill him!"

Simaro offered her a bored smile. *There was no mercy in his winter-blue gaze.*

Staring at him in sheer despair, she prepared to fight. She knew she could not stand here and not try: she'd floor the guards on either side of her. *Easily.* Get to Simaro in less than a blink and-

"Mistress, do not!" Angemar's voice was a violent command across the pit, fording her anguish, "You will tell me not to come searching you, but I will fail to heed your warning: it will be no other way for I can give you hope. Trust me: there will be another time to fight! For now: watch and remember!"

"No," she growled again at Simaro, weighted by harrowing guilt, "You are a flecking Knights Commander! The Protector and Defender of the Western Realm! Where is your Zanzierian honour? Come to your senses, now! Where is the sanctity of your Oaths?!"

Folding his arms, Simaro shook his head, turning slightly as if preparing to enjoy the spectacle. By now the first Demonai was lifting its head, looking straight at Angemar with a hiss and the older man seemed to shiver with fatigue, or fear, or-

"One:-"Angemar's voice rang out, catching her attention like a slap in the face, forcing her not to ignore him, "-to live, you must control

91

your fear. They will feed off it, like energy - then throw it right back at you. Don't let them!"

Solancei shivered. *This was not how it was supposed to go!* Already, the second Demonai raised its head. It did not growl but a line of condensed sliver dribbled from its lips as it zeroed in on Angemar with a predatory glimmer of purpose.

The vision turned Solancei's wrath to water. *Dear Gods. No! No-*

Angemar shivered; as if in tandem both creatures pushed a step forward.

"Two:-" His eyes bored into hers, too intense despite the distance, "-they exude fear: like a stench in the air. It's used to petrify their victims, but it's a ruse - like a courtesan's clever use of perfume to instil a certain mood. If you ignore it, they cannot use it against you. Hyatt'Raah are bred-killers sure but they are not very intelligent. Remember this!"

As if to punctuate his words, the smaller Demonai launched a hesitant swipe towards his flank, but he was yet out of reach and did not honour it a look.

Continuing his rant, he called, "Three: if you come at them confidently, they get confused sometimes long enough for you to cut them down or escape them. Remember this!"

Angemar was shivering now; she could see the sheen of moisture upon his forehead and sense his determination. The Demonai were hissing like snakes as they flickered closer, straining to break through his last reserves. He must know they would succeed any moment now and yet his eyes stayed on her.

Solancei bit her lip in fear.

"Four-" he yelled, his voice raked by a treble of anxiety though he was hefting the butch seax, "-their hide is thick: resistant to injury

92

and harder to penetrate than sheet iron. Only Kaisor-forged Dragon Silver will kill them! Remember this!"

He quivered, eyes straying, "Five-"

Five never came.

With a rattle of chain and a wrenching sound of menace, the first Hyatt launched itself straight at Angemar with elastic fluidity: the sickle claws laying him open from groin to sternum with a terrible precision of a predator desperate for a kill.

The soft illumination failed, throwing a new cover of shadows over the unfolding grisly event.

It was perhaps just the same. Solancei's knees nearly buckled from under her. *Angemar's rising scream was unlike anything she had ever heard as both creatures fell on him to the sounds of cloth ripping - only it might not have been just cloth...*

Silence fell across the cavern abruptly but not a blink too soon - the butchered man's final whimpers ending on a note of surreal choking. However, almost as abruptly the unreal peace was shattered once more, this time by the low, utterly repulsive sound of cracking bones. The Hyatts had begun to feast!

It hardly mattered.

Training or no, Iambre's life-shield or no, Solancei could not get the agonising sounds of Angemar's pain out of her head. *As she stood there it danced a merry good jig with the image of him shivering from the poisons in his body, and she just could not make the Link work to smooth it over. She just could not...*

Ina Uttorian's Reassurances

Iambre, Heiress and Princess of the Realm, stared into the mirror upon the bureau-temporarily-elected 'vanity table'. With more mind on her internal reflections, her eyes did not really see and her own image did not interest her anyway.

It was still early and this evening's spectaculars ongoing in the Knights Hall of Castle Zanzier, yet she had feigned a headache after only a few hours of opulent entertainment. The 'dreadful' malady, combined with a claim that she wanted to attend the festivities of the following nights feeling rested, had allowed her to withdraw quickly and seemingly without offence.

She yawned, vision further blurring. As expected, there had been plenty of well-wishers and sympathisers to see her 'off'. Apparently, headaches were a very common affliction amongst the ladies here, and - seeing matters from a woman's perspective - Iambre thought of the would-be curiosity with lacking surprise. When it came to the question of male/female equality, the Zanzierian mentality was at best tedious, at worst pompous-edging-towards-detestable, and since she was not well-versed in the 'intricacies' of conducting herself like 'the doll', the atmosphere had yet to mellow past 'awkwardly' intense.

Tired beyond ruffled sensitivities, she wondered how these people did this... *this dance of veiled insult and derogatory comments to fuel a lady's lust for violence.* Did their own women not see it? Did they not see or hear the spoken 'unspoken' when it was flashed like poor comedy before their faces. Sadly she thought they did, but elected to ignore; they had an odd code in this place - *the women, a pride of sorts* - and as she'd seen elsewhere: outsiders could not contest the habits of others. It ever ended poorly.

But perhaps she was unfair? She made her eyes focus, mindful of the unattractive frown her mother might have tried to discourage.

'A little rest would doubtlessly find her recovered soon enough' - such had been the general consensus amongst the dour Zanzierian ladies, yet for a wonder, she had also spied just a handful of canny looks directed her way. It had convinced her that at least a few of these ingratiating puppets knew the truth and might even have used similar ploy on occasion.

It brought hope. Of a sort. But old ways died hard. Simply from the way many a lady continued to pale and sympathise - *believing Iambre's plight without 'compare' just because she'd been forced to travel this far from home without a male relation to control and oversee affairs'* - it was obvious that the perception of that which was considered socially acceptable, had not shifted a bean since forever.

Old age still far removed and concerns of wrinkles hardly pressing, her brow tightened. *Her mother 'the queen' would not be proud, but perhaps Queen Ishjah 'the woman' might have been understanding...*

Iambre had given up trying to 'explain' herself midway through last night. Even were she the Heiress, the concept that a woman could be trusted to lead was regarded an absurdity here and it was blatantly clear that even if these ladies knew how to snatch a small freedom here and there, they still had Zanzierian blood and tradition flowing in their veins.

Trying... it was so trying.

Iambre squeezed her eyes shut for a blink. She suspected she confused them: the men with her seeming endless opinions and opposing questions; the ladies, because they did not know where to 'shelve' her. *And she'd been reigning herself back as well, adhering to the council of both Ina and Ambassador Vettaran, not to mention that of Chief Eso!*

Hah, but Zulavi's initial slight seemed nothing now. There were so many things these people could potentially 'choose' to take offense of: her show of confidence, which sat at odds with her gender; her forward manner, voicing disagreement on any matter ranging from the percentage of taxes placed on wine, to the serf-like conditions of the local peasants - *and as for holding a man's eye...*

She made them squirm though. Because they too at least realised that she, in turn, could also take offence of them - and courtesy of her title that still meant something.

Iambre suppressed a huff under her breath. The Zanzierians were her people as much as those of any other province, but they would never be her favourite. Those who *tried* still floundered between stiff and stunted, whilst others seemed oblivious to how many times they blundered. Indeed, remaining civil had become a tip-toe along an edge of hot coals - sometimes not a very elegant display - but at least she was becoming very versatile 'granting amnesty'. *Very...*

She groaned at the compromise, cupping her forehead in her hands. *Delicate flower; ignorant of worldly matters; fragile humours; lacking in years; too tall; not enough persuasion...*

Apparently, she was anything but 'capable'. Sadly, the less she spoke, the better they seemed to like her: she'd seen it in their eyes, read it in their manners and heard it shared without reserve whenever the nuances of their casual small talk and blatant innuendo had not been sufficiently veiled. *Yes... a trying people indeed! Ignorance was not the word!*

96

She swiped one of Palea's left-over sweetmeats from a tiny tiered silver tray nearby and shoved it in her mouth. Chewing vigorously to get to the cherry inside - not really caring for the flavour but forcing herself to swallow - she shoved another one in, chewing hard as though she could somehow grind her vexation to dust.

Oh, but it was a poor day indeed when she must act like a fourteen-summers old girl rather than the person she ought to be. It wasn't good enough! She was skilled at finding some kind of redeeming factor to excuse the various bizarre ideas or habits she'd encounter whilst visiting the provinces – after all, people had a right to nurture their own customs and traditions: it was the very thing that helped the Treaty of Unity survive, but here?

The Zanzierians behaved like selfish bores and their opinions failed inspiration. *Precocious, unyielding, militant...* Gods... was that what the last remaining families of power - the Patricians, the Valdérans and the Sihnarians - had hoped to preserve at the end of the Chaos Wars? Was it what they'd foreseen when they'd reached out to the surviving fourteen states and had encouraged them to join this emerging new world out of an understanding that solidarity and democracy would serve them all better than what had gone before?

Iambre had to admit, she was a little disappointed. Somehow she'd hoped to find Zanzier just a little less reserved than rumour suggested; after all, it had been centuries of integration - but phew! The centuries might as well have been days and with what she'd experienced so far, she found it ever-hard to picture the Zanzierian people part of any common cause other than their own.

Yet it was what it was. No matter if it was almost as bad as the Kheltian stubborn insistence that no man was allowed to remain unmarried after the age of twenty-five, or the Kerikonese arrogant

97

belief that they were the Gods' chosen people and therefore more deserving of... *well, everything.* Yes even then, these people had a right to their past - and future.

Iambre rubbed her temples with her fingertips, then rolled her eyes in self-mockery. Well, she always prided herself on being open-minded and she'd just have to remain so about the Zanzierian way of life, too! In her opinion though, the male-dominated province seemed in bad need of an overhaul, but that was - *of course* - only her opinion, and as expected, now the trained diplomat within, raised finger in caution.

Her visit was not supposed to be of a political nature and she'd have to repress these urges or else risk a heap of ill-will against the throne! Whether or not a province needed to address internal issues, was a discussion for the Senate, not the Crown. *And she'd better recall!*

"My Lady? If I may speak boldly...?"

Gaze focusing, Iambre paused her fingers. Her lady and handmaiden, Ina Uttorian, was marching towards her in the mirror, crossing the bedroom floor like a motherly matron on a mission, apparently not minding her pace even if the tray she wielded was stacked with the pot of steaming tea and china service requested. Without waiting for the by-your-leave that would normally rule them in public, the handmaiden spoke simply as she walked, "Dear grace, in all of my life I have rarely been amongst a larger bunch of stunted, sycophantic idiots! Rarely! And given my position that says a lot!"

Reaching her Mistress, Ina set the tray down with a tiny clatter. Lips curdling, she began to unfasten pins from her gauze veil, rapidly plucking at each gem-faced fastener with the unerring skill that came with repetition.

98

The small precise action reminded Iambre of a chicken plucking corn: peck, peck, peck, although this chicken never allowed herself a breath as she continued to scatter her own dark opinions like a handful of wizened rose petals thrown into the wind.

"I mean, I've heard the rumours like everyone else, My Lady; I've seen the documents, and Gods... I told you my fears didn't I, but still?"

Ina shook off the veil. "Ughh!"

With a vehement shiver as if touched by the cool showers that latched against the windowpanes behind the heavy drapes, she let her long braid swing free to dangle like a bell rope down her back.

Iambre felt the corner of her mouth quiver. Long since used to Ina's forward style, she allowed the older woman to deposit her load - pins and all - on the corner of a chaise lounge right inside the bedchamber.

Though inspired she might feel to commiserate, yet Iambre deemed it best not to comment lest she should find herself unable to stop her own tirade from spilling out. Ina, however, wasn't done.

"Four times I've been groped! Four!" With a disbelieving sniff, the handmaiden snatched her veil back up and continued to fold the length of see-through lilac fabric with angry methodical disregard. "Oh but I swear I'll dust my dress with ground-up heinar and then let's see how quickly they might learn to keep their filthy wandering hands to themselves! Truly My Lady... are they nobles or riff-raff?"

"Well Mistress Uttorian, you tell me?" Iambre injected sweetly and Ina trailed off, finally lifting her eyes to hers. Patiently sliding her elbow onto the vanity table and resting her chin on the palm of her hand, Iambre offered her an arched look, still secretly biting her tongue.

Collecting herself, Ina sucked in a deep breath. Shrugging from her silken surcoat, folding it with a little too much attention to every move, the handmaiden slowly draped the garment across the back of the chaise lounge. Holding her carefully collected breath for a blink longer, the unhappy woman released it. "My Lady, apologies! I rant and I am too forward now! It's unseemly."

Iambre scratched the tip of her nose with a little finger, momentarily bowing her head to hide a wry smile. Looking up she said, "Yes dear Mistress Ina Uttorian, I believe it is... forward,-" the wry smile widened to a genuine grin, "-and still you will probably hear no reprimand from my lips."

"Oh Highness..." Ina smiled sheepishly to show wide neat teeth in appreciation of Iambre's tiny ploy. In more rueful tones, she remarked, "Phew, but that was a trial, was it not? Tell me My Lady thinks the same."

"I think a lot of things, and all of them probably worse than you care to hear," Iambre admitted with a sigh and slid her arm back off the table to flop back in the chair. Folding her hands in her lap she looked up as the handmaiden drew to her side.

She couldn't keep quiet. "Ina, you did not really get... *get groped?* Did you?"

The other woman hesitated, a glimmer of amusement flittering through her eyes. "Ah, My lady..."

Lifting the pot to serve the tea, yet managing to roll her hooded, cosmetically enhanced eyes, Ina snorted softly under her breath. "Your Grace, I well may have been a little rash in my choice of words there. Gods, I did not really say 'grope', now did I, because... well, My Lady knows me, and I..."

Knowing what was coming, Iambre watched the hypnotic flow of golden tea as Ina slowly poured. "You what?"

"Well in Your Grace's world, it would most certainly have been a grope, and in Palea's probably full robbery of her virginity, but alas in mine?" Ina looked pointedly at the china cup as the hot beverage strained into it, and for a beat, Iambre thought she was not going to speak. Then the handmaiden grimaced with a touch of self-conscious chagrin rarely seen. "Well in truth... the insult is on them, Your Grace. Gods, but the foul idiots cannot even get anything *that basic* right!"

Adding a generous dollop of honey to the drink, Ina offered a wide-eyed Iambre the cup with an impish smile, then cleared her throat like an actress to enhance the spoken words, and though Iambre was used to the older woman's ways, for a moment she couldn't seem to speak as she realised what her handmaiden was in fact saying.

"You are complaining that they *did not* grope you right?" she finally managed, cheeks colouring. She steadied the full cup with both hands, trying not to notice how Ina's now indignant frown crafted creases where normally none might be seen. A tiny grimace later Ina crinkled up her delicate bulbous Patrician nose just once and Iambre understood that she'd hit the nail.

"Oh Gods what shall I do with you?" she sighed at length - partly in jest, though she was stirring her tea just a little too vigorously.

"Who knows?" Ina quipped. "Maybe My Lady will thank me after her wedding night one day."

In spite of herself, Iambre snorted with mirth. "Well you know that'll be the day, all right! Now hush about wedding nights and groping and pour yourself some tea."

Ina gave her a gracious nod in thanks and complied whilst Iambre regarded her through lowered lashes wondering why she liked this woman so much. Ina's promiscuous ways were known to her but rarely discussed quite so openly. *Ina had a past: most people had an inkling it was so.* In truth, the argument of whether this woman was anything but 'proper company' had been extensively turned and dissected by a number of advisors, before the verdict on Mistress Uttorian compromising manners had come back with the single word 'disqualified' written in red ink across the name.

That had suited her mother, had suited Lancei too, but not Iambre! Indeed still not sure if Ishjah had arranged for certain money to roll into certain hands just to see Ina dismissed, Iambre had spoken tirelessly for the woman. In a companion to travel the realm she'd wanted someone worldly; someone who knew things; someone who'd lived and realised how best to advise her in Patrician matters - and in certain others, as it were. In the end, however, it was probably not *her* avid words, but rather Ina Uttorian herself, that had raised the support needed, and Iambre suspected Lancei was right. *Ina had probably been very generous with her affections in those last weeks of the final selections. Very.*

Still, the woman had conducted herself impeccably since then. *Well... if one did not count wandering eyes and wayward smiles as an offence that was.*

Iambre smiled softly into the china cup as she sipped her steaming beverage with care. *With Ina she got what expected: no more, no less.* If she needed demure, she had Palea; if she wanted friendship, she had Lancei, but Ina...

Well, Ina was like a jack of all trades, and she liked that! *Her mother had wanted her to bring two other women as well.* Iambre had said 'no'! *Her mother had not been impressed...*

"Well, as it were I guess there is some small act of luck attached to all of this," Ina remarked out of nowhere as she pulled a second ornate chair close to Iambre's and lifted her own cup with a grateful sigh for the smell.

"Really?" Iambre blew her tea, "And just what might that be then?"

"Well My Lady is lucky, I guess-", and here Ina's sloping forehead creased inelegantly again before she continued, "-because just for once, Solancei's absence is rather well-timed, is it not? We both know she would suffer, had she to conform to this level of tact; that she...

"Well begging your pardon, but she does not conform well at times, that's all. My Lady did good to land her with temple duties. That way I guess you won't have to gag her."

Cosmetically blue-rimmed lips splitting in a smile to soften the effect of her words, Ina could not know how hard the words hit. The painful urge to punch the forward woman passed in a blink, but not so the hard knot in her chest and Iambre had to fight to appear amused.

With a tractable curve of an eyebrow that seemed to make her face ache for the stiffness it provoked, she managed to sound light-hearted and barely acerbic. "Oh my dear Ina, Solancei can be tactful if needs be. You just have to ask her the right way. Yet..."

Iambre carefully met the handmaiden's eyes. "And yet you speak the truth. Zanzier and its nobles would certainly test her, I fear. Anyway, she's absent, not because I dread her conduct, but because I am trying to convince her that she needs to think twice

103

about leaving me in the lurch again. I think a few days in solitude and meditation may find her able to align her view to mine on this matter, so that's that."

Chief Eso's lie sifted across her lips with sleek persuasion and only a shimmer of guilt that she'd been reduced to lying to her own staff - but it was better than the alternative, for even Ina could not be allowed a whiff of their 'predicament'. Let them all just think that she'd sent Lancei to the temple of Inkar'Chi to ponder her failure to 'appear on duty'. It served a purpose; served to explain Solancei's continued absence with a plausible excuse to placate questions and calm any potential whispers - and in truth, her lies did not seem too far-fetched; she knew how people would talk in corners that it must be high time *Her Highness*, began to reign in *'that'* pesky handmaiden.

'Disrespect of procedures and authority, biting honesty, tardiness and other sorts of wayward behaviour'... those were all the type of disagreeable traits that would reflect poorly on a new queen, she'd been told - and importantly, it would not be tolerated by her peers indefinitely. Still, she paid this little mind, although now...

Well luckily then, this little 'incident' should finally prove to the critics that their Princess was capable of side-setting her 'obvious favouritism' in honour of necessity. Or so she hoped. Smoke and mirrors; smoke and mirrors...

Moved by ill-suspicions, Iambre chewed on the inside of her cheek to dispel with the ugly thoughts, but Lancei missing was like half of herself gone missing!

A shiver rattled her shoulders, but she applied herself brisk cheer to brush away the discomfort. "Ina come! Please, forget about

104

Solancei! What about Palea now? Where did we 'misplace' her, I wonder?"

"My Lady, she was right behind us," Ina told her. "I am sure she will not be long. Perhaps she's gone to get that cool compression I asked her to fetch."

"Yes of course." Iambre knew she sounded absent-minded, and Ina must have heard, for she sat her cup and saucer down.

"My Lady, I would go and find her if you require?" Ina made as if to get up, but Iambre shook her head.

"She will be here soon enough I suspect." Iambre waved a hand at the general idea of everything. "Tell me instead if you would have some pearl of wisdom for how I might proceed without killing my reputation on the morrow?"

"Well allow me to think, now..." Ina grinned, shifting slightly in her seat as though to settle in for the long night and Iambre observed the elegant sway of the woman's long back with a drop of envy. *Ina was naturally lissom and the way in which she moved made the handmaiden thoroughly hard to ignore. No wonder they all wanted to catch her eye...*

The Heiress looked away with deliberate care then and for a moment she envied her handmaiden everything. Not that she craved more attention - no, it wasn't that - but the woman was hypnotising; exotic! *Luscious Ina; beguiling Ina... Ina with her patterns and colours, moulding fabrics and daringly-cut dresses; 'Ina the Bold'.* Yes, the woman seemed to adjust to each new situation as though she was simply browsing through a local market and Iambre envied her the freedom she appeared to embrace without discord or apology. Ina was interesting to people; an enigma of a

105

kind, with just the right amount of the guile that so often accompanied those of supposed secrets.

Still, Ina was honest in a way few people managed; in a way that remained true to her own desires but not to the exclusion of others, and the Princess liked that to spite her Patrician roots, it would seem that Ina Uttorian had gone a long way to honour her Esardan heritage too. Sure, she was an Iddian noble with a shady past and many years estranged from her own family over an issue best forgotten – that much was true – yet Iambre would secretly have swapped places with the woman in a beat. *The past had moulded Ina, and still she'd the courage to carry on.* Iambre hoped that she might eventually sport just a fraction of her mature handmaiden's tenacity; a fraction of her independence. *To be Ina would be easy,* she thought; *to be Ina would be fun; to be Ina would be… well, the opposite of being me!*

"My Lady? You… you look tired." The older woman injected, ripping Iambre back to the present.

"What? Oh… no, it's nothing, I-" Blinking, her gaze yet again decidedly blurry from focussing blindly on the face in the mirror, the Ostravahn Princess stroke the tip of her tongue across still-rouged lips gone dry in spite Palea's earlier machinations with a lanolin concoction.

"My lady, I beg the differ." Ina stood up resolutely. "And as your handmaiden, is it not my responsibility to ensure your well-being? I think we need to get you out of these clothes and wash off this make-up."

Rapidly contemplating her hands, Iambre felt a wave of nuisance roll through her and she bit in a harsh grimace, as for a beat, a part of her rebelled against this relentless farce: this excessive need to

106

repeat the same, day in and day out: *dress, make-up, hair... smile, conform, defer... sleep, eat, repeat... don't fall off the pedestal now!*

None of that was Ina's fault, however, and so she demurred with a small gesture. The sooner she were to bed, the sooner she'd be up, the sooner she could repeat this, the sooner the days would pass to see her closer to the point where she could say good-riddance to this pit of vipers, and the sooner Lancei-

Iambre sat back and refused to think, yet Ina getting busy with her potions and lotions, soft cloths and miniature sponges, felt a curiously strange anti-climax to the day.

Oddly, though the desire was somewhat irrational, she wanted Palea back where she could see the girl. They were all adults here but it seemed to Iambre that Solancei's disappearance had already made her more protective of the other two women, something surely unwarranted in a place like this, except...

Except that Diekima'Chi, dual-faced deity of Lies and Deceit, awaited cunningly disguised in the shadows here: she'd sensed it before arriving. It was not enough either to wield the idea that Zulari'Chi the Wise could usually be found ready to block the canny manoeuvres of His sly brother in these cases, no: Iambre feared they'd all have to watch their backs!

A new shiver ran through her, startling Ina, who - muttering something under her breath - went to fetch a cover for her shoulders; Iambre mumbled thanks, but her chill persisted.

Maybe it was that Zulavi, she pondered, suppressing a new shiver as the rapid pinpricks of rain stabbed against the windows with renewed vigour. Zulavi had arrived late tonight - *very late and armed only with poor excuses!* - but she'd smiled and nodded as though untouched by the performance. *Smiled. And simmered. And planned. And not long after made her excuses to withdraw.*

The memory of the man's face brought a stringent sense of justice. *Tit for tat as she'd told Bilan on the first night. Tit for tat...*

Still, she knew the Knights Commander would need placating as some point - it took no skill to realise this - but with her feelings for Bilan and Solancei to cloud her senses, she hadn't really paid attention to her Lord Host one way or another. *Perhaps that was a mistake but what did she care?*

"So My Lady, how fares your 'headache'?" Ina's quiet words drew her from further thoughts of Zulavi and she was almost thankful.

"Oh I think that we can safely say it's improving by the heartbeat, thank you," Iambre affirmed with a cheeky wink to cheer herself. *Ina knew damn well that the headache thing was bogus, but still... the fact that she might think herself into a real headache before bedtime was a whole other matter entirely! Ina needn't know that part though.*

"So, what did you make of it all, then?" Iambre enquired with a tired sigh, raising an eyebrow as Ina turned the vial of rose oil upside down to wet a cotton flannel. "I mean, really? Could I have acted differently?"

"My Lady as it is, I think it safe to say that you were a picture of perfection." Ina smiled, shook her head in wonder, then relented, "Your Grace should relax. It could've all gone much worse. In all probability, these louts will never be able to acknowledge the fact that you are not a male heir, so trust me: you did well; in fact, someone should give you a medal of valour! My... rather give me a droll Tarléonin any day, than this bunch of sycophants!"

Taking another sip of her tea, timing it so that she could drink in-between Ina' gentle machinations with the cloth, Iambre nodded in accord.

"Oh, I hardly need a medal but your words spread warmth. Inkar'Chi defend, it is no lie that I was dreading tonight; Gods, Ina, how am I to stand another eight days of this without bursting?"

"My Lady, you will endure because you must and because we're within the halls of a powerful ally, who despite other faults, still remains King Kaimar's man without a fail." Ina paused, offering a rueful look. "Now given your status and the need for us to uphold etiquette, I don't think you require me to tell you that there is no real choice whether to attend or not."

Ina eyed the Heiress in the mirror, wringing out a sigh of surrender. *The handmaiden was right but Iambre wished it wasn't so and suddenly she felt glad that she'd asked the older woman to attend the temple of Kira'Cha earlier.* The gold and the incense donated was worth a small fortune and Ina had come back glowing with pleasure: both for the temple's gratitude and for the promised blessings. In return, Iambre now sincerely hoped that the Goddess would throw her several measures of luck to help her endure this 'pit' for the remainder of her visit, but Luck was a fickle thing. *As fickle as they come...*

A small tick pulled at her heart. *Was it too much to hope her offering might also help return Solancei to her side, safe and hale? Was it?*

"My Lady, Kira'Cha was generous with her esteem today." As though she was able to part-guess the subject of her Mistress' thoughts, Ina spoke up then, clearly to comfort as she continued, "Both Her Adepts and the Devine Oracle assured me! My Lady,

109

Luck is by your side to rule your fate as it falls, so don't fear - all *will* be well!"

Iambre nodded to show her agreement but her re-occurring fear over Solancei's disappearance did not make Ina's words seem possible. To avoid questions though, she pushed herself and swept this like-wise re-occurring unease aside. One thing was for certain, she could not keep suffering a headache every night until she was due to travel to her next engagement - not without insulting everyone in attendance at least, and she did not want to be the first to give Zanzier an excuse to take offence! If she had to bite her tongue and smile with a pretty, vacant look in her eyes, then - *death and daffodils* - she would do so, if it meant preserving the diplomatic relations between her station and this province! Lancei was gone; of course, it did not give her permission to simply sit here on her pretty perch and wait, trapped as a wild sparrow in a gilded cage. *There was work to do, but Gods... Solancei! What about Solancei?*

Solancei's Memoirs
The Province of Etruia.
Castle Servangar.
Summer of 800 P. C. W.

The ~~handwrittling~~... the ~~handwottle~~... the written... the... what's the right word, now? The... *the handwriting?* Yes, that's the one!

Okay, yes... so *the handwriting* has turned sloppy. I apologise. I was never the neatest scribe to begin with, but on this occasion I think it safe to say that the reason is indisputably entwined with the fact that red and green twin flacons standing empty on the silver tray on my bureau, now seem to have turned into undulating dancers whenever I happen to glance their way. They have the curves for it - and I, enough alcohol on the inside to appreciate their simple, impromptu entertainment.

Still their presence is a distraction; perhaps I should move the tray over to my left - but then I remember that it will no longer make any difference, so I simply sit here and stare at the beautiful faience inlay around the tray's fluted, raised edge, wondering if this is the newest style at court, or if war and prudence have forced the good King Kaimar to dig out the heirlooms from yesteryear. It is certainly more ornate than the typical Etruian style - but look... here I go again. I digress, though the time is well past the latest hour of the day, and my memories sufficiently dulled so that I can stand to examine them.

I ~~beluve~~... I ~~beleeve~~... *I believe*... I believe my condition is what connoisseurs might call 'tipsy' - it was what I was aiming for certainly - and if it complicates my thought pattern somewhat, I am now also infinitely more prepared to tell you about my enhanced experience in regards to that flecking accident that everyone had sought to shield me from.

I ~~promase~~... I ~~prommis~~... *I promise* that I shall continue forthwith - *although incidentally...*

Did you perchance know that interestingly, the dream that was never really a dream, was the reason I since never liked to set foot, seat or even eye on these vehicles of death? I had to on occasions, of course, but if

111

given the choice, I'd forever shun carriages; I just cannot abide them: they make me-

Ah well...

Anyway, back to the issue at hand. Now, as it were during this unwanted, twisted little piggy-back coach-ride of mine, I was as aware of the smallest sound, as I was of the greatest jolt: aware of every nuance in smells, in colour, in the emotions rolling off the passengers - and so, I even knew something of what went on beyond the carriage walls, although how this was possible?

I... I... well, as I mentioned before, **when the carriage jostled everyone within - I lost that immediate sense of relief that had momentarily led me to believe that the carriage ride was my reality and that the funeral had been the dream. I also mentioned that my joy evaporated on a cutting vibe of 'wrong', sending tendrils of creeping chill and premonition through me that this was not going to end well, but here's the wicked thing...**

Though my senses of reality had been well and truly messed-up, I suddenly didn't care. No matter the bubble of fear in my belly, no matter my sense of imminent disaster, I still wanted to stay. I wanted to stay in that coach; with Taliana; and with my parents; because in that moment they were not dead and if I only stayed, then maybe... *well then maybe they would not die.*

As I recall very well, an exquisite elation rose up on the back of that little idea, smothering my moment of strange lucidity, drenching me with determination. *I no longer cared about reality - or maybe I forgot - because I was next to Taliana. Not dead. And my parents - mother on Taliana's other side, and my father and his valet on the bench opposite. Not dead.*

So I buried the sense of the unreal. My new relief was crushing! Though a voice in the back of my head warned me not to trust this illusion, I stomped it out, contented to leave my idea of a nightmare behind, contented to be here instead, which - in hindsight - would prove to be quite ironic!

112

You see, in the end, I only swopped one terror for another. With my determination, I changed nothing yet somehow it served to embed this very hag-ridden dream in my head so firmly, that I would revisit it upon myself several hundred times over and over till I learned to control the black terror: learned to smother the horror of guilt that kept revisiting, that no matter what, I alone would escape the slaughter, because I alone would wake up, when they did not!

Which God would curse a person to experience such insight?

Well bewildering - as it turned out, and not quite as suspected - no God at all, and not even the State of Veranto either, though for a very long time I thought it definitely so. But then what?

Well, I was a very long time in learning the truth from a man you may sadly never know. *A truth, which I am still struggling to accept as fact, however!* And yes, you will undoubtedly think me somewhat deluded and simple - but there is not a flecking thing that will allow me to write down *those* words until the day I'm ready, because I am still hoping to discover this truth just another lie; I am still hoping to wake up from this 'dream' one day - but of course, it is but a weak fancy of mine and I know it can never be so.

Taliana, and my parents and the others... they all died because of me. Gods hate - I swear... if only I had *really physically* been in that coach all those years ago, things would've panned out very differently. See I always believed that had I been with Taliana and my parents, then I would have been the one to die, and they would've all lived - and it's the truth I told myself for such a long time that I occasionally still believe it so, but-

But with everything I've seen, the lie is golden brass, of course, and I know it.

None of us would've survived. None of us would've stood a chance.

Solancei

113

Too Many Thoughts

Solancei...

The Princess ignored the knot that formed in her chest, closely followed by a spasm that seemed to tighten her ribcage like a corset. She knew no choice but to leave that particular 'headache' for Chief Eso to deal with, but whenever it hit her that her friend was missing, that same strange feeling twisted her guts!

How could she enjoy opulence and glorious entertainment when Lancei's whereabouts and well-being remained an uncertainty? The 'not knowing' tore deeper than any of the incidental insults received from the Zanzierian bootlickers, and though they should have, all of Ina's reassurances did little to appease her. *She did not like this place!* She missed her friend with every beat of her heart and all she had for comfort was Bilan's reassuring words, which still echoed in her mind like a mantra to keep her inner peace afloat.

Gods, but without Lancei, Bilan seemed the only link to safety within these walls and even that remained flimsy. The Keep was huge. Bilan might as well have been all the way back in Etruia already for how far away he felt to her.

A subtle stinging in her nose brought water to her eyes, regret and bad conscience still at war. She'd miss Bilan an awful lot, yet how it was possible to still feel this way with Lancei gone Gods knew where? *Did that make her a bad friend that her mind and feelings were split between the two people?*

Iambre bit her lip, dragging her teeth across it and barely registering Ina's reprimand. *Was it wrong that Bilan was in her heart too, and that a whole day seemed such a long time not seeing him?*

Well, Lancei clearly believed so, but in a heated flash that made her heart bounce, she remembered her and Bilan's wildly inappropriate embrace the night before. *What was it again, that had made her choose to send him home? It seemed a stupidly daft promise now.*

A hard inhale that shifted everything deep within her core earned her Ina's scrutiny in the mirror but she distilled the woman's concern with tiny gesture and a small exclamation to lay blame on fatigue. As ever Iambre lacked the word to describe the feelings in her heart but in the aftermath of chaotic emotions and longing, she'd had to face the same, rather disconcerting, truth over and over. *She could not run! The man turned her head to mush and the rest of her-*

Gods but Solancei believed her stubborn, yet as Princess and Heiress, Iambre hadn't deliberately set out to throw her heart away to one of her father's soldiers. The very thought might seem romantic, but in reality...

How had she come to this? In truth, she did not want him to have that effect on her! *She really didn't!* Every time she saw him: gone was the sensible, considerate Crown Princess and in her stead, this gooey-brained half-wit person appeared; a person without thought for Crown or future; a person sadly filled with nothing but a string of filthy ideas more in keeping with a common taproom wench, than a prim, educated Lady who should know better! *Oh, it was moon-shot, but Bilan had been right. If he would not leave her thoughts, he'd have to leave her presence, but...*

Emotions rising anew, Iambre blinked rapidly and Ina mumbled an apology for getting too near her eyes.

She'd promised to de-commission him. So she would. Only, the thought of not seeing him anymore made her sick. *Bilan...*

115

wonderfully uncomplicated; every inch of him was just right! Warm sun-darkened skin just a shade deeper than golden leather, his weirdly crooked nose and softly curling hair devastating assets, and his eyes...

His near-black eyes sported flecks the colour of old oak: flecks, which she could only really see when she stood close enough to kiss him; Bilan...

At the very thought of what she wanted to do with him, her heart somersaulted with delight and Iambre clenched her hands together under the cover, hoping Ina would believe that her cheeks turning scarlet was to do with the cleansing regime. *It was not right, not right at all - and yet it was! And that was why he would be leaving!*

Iambre sucked in a gulp of air, beset all at once both with longing and guilt. She knew she ought to have done this 'deed' ages ago; Lancei had bid her a hundred times over to consider, to understand, to wake up! And yes, she'd known her friend right: she had to let him go! But she hadn't wanted to. And yes, being told had only made her more obstinate. And yes...

Yes, yes, yes! Lancei hadn't even been unreasonable - her pleas that Iambre should ship him off and move on, were wonderfully rational, based on objective fears and impeccable loyalty, but Gods...

Her father had thought it such an excellent decision to place Bilan in charge of her safety whilst she travelled to Tuxama! *What would he think or say when he suddenly found Bilan returned to him without suave reason? It had not been a great excuse to ignore Lancei, but an excuse it had been...*

Not knowing of the tumult that went on within her Mistress, Ina misread the silence and laid a warm hand on Iambre's forearm, again so as to comfort. "My Lady, Kira'Cha will not abandon us. All

116

will be well - you'll see. Soon we will leave here and when the moon turns black twice from now, you will have reached Tuxama and then you'll be able to rest. Dear Gods, My Lady knows I adore adventures, but even I must confess that a return to routine will be as welcome as a warm shelter on a winter's night. It's been a long year!"

"Yes, I know it has," Iambre replied, humouring Ina all the while feeling the ever-present knot in her chest flex to grow harder. *The thought of Tuxama held no welcome in her heart. None at all.* She wished that she could ask for Bilan to be there but...

"I know,-" she repeated because she was expected to, "-and we're all tired. A return to normality will be welcome. Eleven full moons on the road will do that to anyone, I guess."

Ina cast her a small smile of agreement, "I guess, Highness. And Zanzier is tedious. Nothing but old fortifications and even older views about the world and its set-up. Again allow me to stress you do well to abide their opinions with such immaculate grace. I believe your father would commend you."

"Perhaps." Iambre allowed, but her mind was not really connecting with the pleasantly safe path Ina's platitudes appeared to be taking and the handmaiden must have sensed her mood, for she fell blessedly silent once more then.

Bilan, Zanzier, Zulavi, Tuxama, Lancei... so many fears and questions; so little ability to affect a single thing! Her mother would have pinched her to snap her mind back to reality; would have warned her to recall what was important; what had to be important! And of course - only one thing was: Tuxama. *Tuxama, and nothing else!*

The knot in her chest became a ball: *squeezing...*

117

It was the same clenching feeling that would arise on and off over the years since she'd reached thirteen summers of age, and having managed to cope very well recently, she felt a spike of alarm at the development. Her own fears would fester if she let them. Fester and rot her peace of mind and common sense until she could not breathe and passed out.

Wise-woman Riselta called the episodes 'panic infection', and perhaps the medic was right. As always though, it led Iambre back to the same old point of rebellion; the rebellion against her mother and against her own 'glorious destiny and duty' as Princess Heiress of the Realm.

Well rats to the lot! Had she asked for this? No!

Did she want this? No!

Did anyone comprehend? No! Well... except for Lancei, but even her cousin did not truly understand!

She tried not to picture all the things her mother might argue 'Iambre did not comprehend', and pushed to rid herself of the mental images of Ishjah trying to prepare her for a life she'd never really been able to embrace the idea of. *If she hadn't been an only child, then maybe, but... but there was really no escaping it though, and maybe it was not such a bad thing, but it meant her never really just belonging to herself; it meant-*

With a bitter twist of her mouth, Iambre wrenched her mind back to the man she knew she was not allowed to love. She couldn't think of Lancei missing; she did not want to think of Tuxama - then better to keep her mind on the subject of Captain Metavo! At least he was not lost to her... *yet.*

It was a disaster, but it wasn't. He wanted to do right by her; she understood better now exactly how much so and why - but still...

118

Of course, the never-forgotten barrier of duty and titles would always stand between them, but this altered few facts of her heart. When she was with him it all seemed a fog of smoke and mirrors that made the consequences of today fall out of context with tomorrow. It was a false blessing, she knew, and it had made her feel twice the monster, recently. And no, there was little about this affair to be proud about. Indeed, she abhorred how little by little she had grown into a caricature of her former self; how she had spawned into someone everyone now failed to recognize - including her own best friend.

A twitch of worry for Lancei's whereabouts returned and she wished she'd not been so impossible. *For Solancei had not been blind nor deterred. Her old friend had seen behind the veneer long ago; had seen how it really was - and wasn't it true that right from that day in Camporia - perhaps even before - Iambre had known she wanted Bilandro Metavo, at first as an ideal, but then...*

She shuddered, the embarrassment deepening. She had ever gotten what she wanted, the perks of her station had never lacked bounty, yet in the beginning, at least she'd questioned the morality of her sentiment for Bilan. At least, in the beginning, she'd recalled her honour, but then somewhere between what she'd wished for and what she'd wanted, the lines had begun to blur, and then...

What was wrong with her?! Bilandro Metavo had not been some parrot or a fine bolt of fabric that she could simply point at and have delivered; she was not that deluded, but then again...

She hadn't thought it possible to ever find herself in such an impossible fix either, and Lancei had been right! *Too bloody right!* And so she'd treated them both like garbage; treated everyone like garbage, and wasted her own precious time; and now they were but

119

two new moons from reaching Tuxama where - *unlike the Lance Captain of her father's personal guard, Bilandro Metavo* - 'destiny and duty' would have *her* firmly planted for the next two years!

Iambre quivered, a light-headed feeling swooping over her, but she couldn't help it. This... this would be her last bit of scheming; her last little revolt before the inevitable. And so help her any deity willing to listen and forgive, but she would send Bilan away - *just like Lancei wanted; just like she must!*

Feeling trapped, full of shame and full of regret for how she'd conducted herself and how she'd allowed Lancei to absorb too much wrap on her behalf, Iambre exhaled a sigh hearty enough to earn a perturbed look off Ina.

"My Gods... where is that girl Palea?" she heard her handmaiden mumble as she twisted the stopper out of the final vial to complete the routine.

"Ina, it's no matter. I think this will do." Iambre injected just shy of snapping. The words were barely out before she recognised her own brass behaviour, but by then an apology would sever Ina's silence and it would be asking for questions she could not answer.

"As My Lady wishes." Ina acknowledged smoothly as she replaced the stopper and set the bottle back into its appropriate compartment of the box they shared for these rituals. Stepping aside, she motioned for Iambre to stand and she obliged, woodenly shifting, raising and lowering limbs when the older woman demanded, waiting patiently in-between the handmaiden secreting her pieces of wardrobe back into the correct coffers and trunks. *It should have been Lancei doing this. Ina usually did the mornings on account of Lancei 'running errands' whilst really actually busy training...*

Iambre bit her lip, pulling it between her teeth. It wasn't like she'd never admitted this to herself before, but yet again it struck her just how much she needed Lancei to tell her to 'snap her royal stupidity out of it'! It might irk her to the roots but Lancei was also impossible to ignore.

At the thought, the tightness in her chest seemed to double. Gods help her: it seemed she could not waylay concerns for long, no matter what. *Not thinking of Lancei, she did exactly that! But her cousin had to be fine!* Because that's what Chief Eso had promised and so, by default and reputation, that's what would happen! *The Chief did not make pledges that would not keep in the face of reality. Never. Chief Eso would find Lancei and when she did, they'd have words and everything would be better!*

Iambre eyed Ina as she returned from hanging up the long detachable sleeves of her blue gown. The handmaiden seemed carefully neutral in the face of her mistress' bizarre mood, but Iambre knew she had the woman puzzled; Ina was not above asking about these things, but today she seemed to know not to push and Iambre was thankful. She did not enjoy telling her ladies these small lies about Solancei and she knew she must elaborate if Ina was to receive a satisfactory answer. *Gods but she wished Bilan was here. Right now. Wished that it was him undressing her...*

Iambre scowled at the floor, feeling less than proud. Between thick worries about her missing handmaiden, and the steamy dreams of Bilan that seemed to pop up at the most random times like an epidemic she couldn't fight inside her head, she did not know where to put her thoughts. The two most important people in her life seemed intertwined right now - not in the common sense of the word but in the spiritual. With Lancei not around, there were possibilities for her and Bilan to meet on a more intimate footing, yet how could she even think to invite such a scenario when her cousin might be injured or worse. Lancei missing did not lower her longing for Bilan, but her conscious could see no way for her to enjoy the luck, and it occurred to her that Kira'Cha might very well be laughing heartily right now. *Luck indeed. Be careful what you ask for... For ask you did, didn't you?*

Momentarily put out that she'd been to blame for this, Iambre swallowed hard. *How often had she wished for Lancei to drop dead for an hour or two, just-*

For there had been other times of course; times and places where she'd had similar hankerings and where she'd thought of sneaking off to find Bilan, only it had rarely panned out quite right. For starters, Solancei-blasted-hawk-eye-Calverhana had usually guessed the truth behind her friend's need to make an 'unscheduled' sally and had put a stop to it accordingly. On other occasions, Lancei had simply smiled innocently and told her that she'd of course accompany *Her Grace.*

Iambre tried to avert a cringe.

With Solancei humming in the background and offering them knowing glances whenever they got within four feet of each other, those 'chaperoned' meetings between her and Bilan had just been plain embarrassing. They had met, of course, stolen the odd moments together on other occasions; occasions where Lancei had either been busy with Eso, bed-ridden, or 'off-duty' - but those one-to-one meetings had never gone far: there'd been a promise that it would, but all the same, it had never happened. *Between Bilan's contrition and propriety and Lancei's echoing words of warning, caution and sense had usually severed the situation of serious* romance as effectively as standing next to a dung heap might have done - and if it had left both her and the Captain wanting, then...

Iambre spun to allow Ina access to her girdle. Somehow, she hadn't thought Zanzier the place to go changing her stars. *Was this all in her head or had the Goddess played a cruel joke on them all?*

Castigating her own superstition, she tried to relax. *Did Kira'Cha expect her to jump for joy?* She smiled at the idea. *Even had she felt tempted to go find Bilan on her own, her knowledge of Zanzierian propriety would've held her back.*

Dear Gods, it wasn't even as if she could just go trudging around the place, anyway. For one, where to start? She'd be spotted within a heartbeat and doubtlessly given an escort, which would then ruin everything as well as any foray with Solancei in tow. *If she spent just a heartbeat contemplating the issue of how to circumnavigate the problem and make good on an old, very inappropriate, very fey promise to herself, it was just a heartbeat, nothing more. And she would certainly never... never...*

Still, Bilan brought her calm. When everything was not steeped in cheap indecent longings, his presence was like peace and she wished she had that feeling now: peace to deal with Lancei's absence and Bilan's imminent departure, peace to deal with the Knights Commander and how best to abide his company in the days to come.

Her chest tightened.

Suddenly impatient to the core, Iambre stepped away from Ina before she could loosen the strings enough to relieve her of the girdle but Iambre pulled at the thing, drawing it over her head in a scrambled well of hair, metal and cotton.

"My Lady," Ina protested with a deepening sigh that neared a huff of exasperation, but Iambre simply dumped the thing on a chair, not caring if ribbons twisted and strands of golden hair lingered in the filigree.

"Just leave it," she commanded as the woman stooped to tidy and the handmaiden bend her neck minutely as she obliged with a smooth manoeuvre that almost covered the disconcerting feel of the frown that momentarily appeared on her forehead, then disappeared.

"Ina, you should go and get some rest. Palea can finish up when she comes." Looking back from the large oval of polished silver, the image of Iambre's smooth skin and large eyes seemed to mock her attempted serenity and her chest contracted a fraction more. In the reflection, she saw Ina's face contort like she was staring at a puzzle, searching for the right anchor piece to proceed, but then the lady offered her a quick curtsy and ghosted from the chamber a lot more quietly than she'd arrived.

For a moment longer, Iambre perused the floor with unseeing eyes. Without even the slightest hint of warning, her stomach dropped, the dizziness she hadn't known in such a long time suddenly rolling over her like slow, ominous thunder from the hills of Ariana's Daughters.

With a small sound of disbelief, she staggered. *Suddenly the floor spun...*

Balance awry, she bumped the chair, jolting the table. It set beauty products and tea service rattling with a delicate ring of glass and china against china, curiously loud one blink only to fade as though she was going deaf. The room tilted oddly, like the deck of a ship gently straining against fresh wind and waves, but it was speeding up, the waves becoming harder and the swaying... *faster...*

A fork of panic stabbed through her innards as her body reacted with urgency, tightening her breath and twisting her guts. *Dear Gods... she'd not suffered a panic infection in months! Not now, dear Gods, not-*

Snatching out blindly, her hand found the back of the carved chair she'd occupied, but as her fingers closed on the frame, Iambre had no notion of anything but the tightening in her chest. Her breath constricted. She tried for a new breath, but the air had gone thick; it wouldn't pass through her windpipe, it wouldn't-

Seeing pinpricks of darkness close in over her vision like whirling tornadoes, she felt an odd spiralling sensation and her body went loose. Then darkness slammed into her like a warhorse attacking an opponent at a joust, but it felt not violent, only instant, then-

Solancei's Memoirs
The Province of Tarléon.
Hilt's pass; westbound.
Autumn of 780 P. C. W.

So I was on the seat next to Taliana. It cushioned my hind, its plush leather padding still good though wear had put a patina of shine and cracks across the once-lush suede, blighting the russet colour to a dark rusty hue that reminded me of the flush that adorns the belly feathers of a Kheltian carrion crow. The dark timber panels seemed to draw what little light there was: absorbing it. Outside cracked a whip with hard demand; once, twice, thrice...

The carriage hit another pothole: deeper now, sending everyone nearly off their seats, though the adults had all latched on to the twisted lengths of faded rope that was attached to the carriage walls to act as hand-grips in case one needed to steady oneself in just such an eventuality. I noticed my mother's knuckles shining skeletal white underneath her faded, pallid skin as she gripped the looping rope: the death-lock of a person too preoccupied by circumstances to concern herself with the pain of cloth-burn or the cramp of overwrought fingers unused to such wear.

The whip cracked again: a sound too loud. There was this glossy artificial sense about everything, a sense of too much colour and yet not enough light, and I myself seemed to have become brittle: shards of my person had begun to flake off as though I couldn't keep the layers tight enough to stop this unformed, imaginary chisel from working them lose. The four adults shared the space in a constrained silence, which seemed to eat all warmth from the air. That was also wrong. My father's face was pinched narrow; somehow out of shape - like that of a snow riz, the dog-sized rodents that would creep into the bowels of Ivanor to winter near the heat of the castle furnaces and be a part-nuisance/part-terror to the workers. On occasion, they'd kill a man, but mostly they'd just intimidate everyone with their size and presence as they cut long groves into the foundations with their teeth and splintered the bones of dead prisoners as though in play. The snow riz would grow bigger in response to threat and so would my father usually, but in his coach on this fateful day, his large frame looked smaller than I'd ever seen, the red of his weather-beaten cheeks as ruddy and fine veined as ever, but now also a sharp, unhealthy contrast to his waxy eastern complexion. He ignored me now. They all did. I felt hot and clammy at the same time, this intangible anxiety gnawing, but Taliana was there, so...?

Rising within me, a curious sensation flowed like water up my gullet. A certain sense of displacement followed: somehow a gagging restraint - and for a few short blinks new disorientation made my head spin, although not as badly as the motion provoked by the vehicle as it rocked precariously along the mildly snow-swept route.

Snow swept? How did I know it was snow swept? How did I know that the ground had recently been covered by three inches of new dusty snow: the fluffy kind, lacking moisture...?

In truth, I do not know - or rather: these days I do! See in truth my stunning understanding was simply caused by the exact same 'thing' that had 'blessed' me with this unwanted insight in the first place - but that is not what I wish to think about now, so let's leave that for another time.

On the seat next to me Taliana shifted uncomfortably, the escaped wisps of her red hair floating with the usual charming disregard for the tight plaits that framed the warm bronze of her Iddian cheeks - just as I remembered. Like father, she seemed a paler shade of herself though, her skin tinted sallow by what I knew must be a combination of emotions and the weather. I had never seen Taliana treading water with fear before; it stirred my emotions anew, though in honesty her familiar face still momentarily served to waylay and distract. I knew something puzzled me though, and so I tried to speak. *Then I tried again. And again.*

Not being able to utter a sound when you really need to, carries its own punishing horror. A desperation grew in me, as I tried and tried but could no more manage a sound than had I been just a mute spirit. I simply could not speak and for some reason, Taliana did not really seem to care. Or maybe she just didn't notice in her heightened state of honed distress? In any event, I don't know why she did not seem to acknowledge me with her usual alacrity and warmth, but I swear I felt as though she wanted me far away from herself at that moment: far away from the carriage and my parents.

I relented and gave up trying to speak then.

Well... maybe not 'gave up', in as much as I sat tight for a moment whilst I tried to figure out what to do instead. The coach moved in a way that made my belly swirl and I suppressed the need to heave, staring blindly at the hand-carved patterns across the narrow door as though the tiny leaping fox-creatures and lines of stars and shapes held the answers to my dilemma. A mouthful of fresh, ice-lanced air would have been nice to settle my queasy tendencies, but the thick swags of custom-made brocade were tied down tight to the metal bar below the thick antique Tuxaman glass panes, thus preventing me from actualising the deed.

I was not old, or wise, nor particularly insightful for my age, but Taliana had drilled me into thinking about my surroundings in a way that might have seemed odd to any child not of Tarléonin stock, however, to us it was done as part of our schooling and as part of our understanding of the province's many sly dangers. And so it was that it occurred to me then that the blinds might have been tied for more than sheer physical comfort; that it also served to visually protect the carriage travellers from that which transpired on the outside.

That notion cooled my blood. I realised it could be night or day - on a whim I thought it night-time - yet of the two sets of hexagonal brass lanterns flanking the doors, only a single one had been lit and the wick turned low. It seemed odd, but there could be several reasons for that of course. Firstly, it might not be night at all; secondly, it might not have been deemed necessary to light up the insides when no one was attempting to read or weave or tally calculations, but in my backbone I knew it was something else: a third reason as of yet unsolidified, but valid. Once more the deep, woollen silence pressed itself again me like a physical thing

128

trying to squeeze the fluid from my body and crush the bones in my limbs. The coach tilted sharply as the driver took the team around a sloping corner without slowing and I saw father's throat work as he swallowed hard.

Why were we going at this speed? The snow masked many a sound, but I could hear the metal rimmed wheels of our vehicle sing a dull song of urgency as they cut over the surface without mercy and the escorting housecarls rode close, the hooves of their stout but fit, weather-hardened ponies falling like a rapid staccato drumbeat that could just be picked out below that of our driver's whip and the sounds coming off our carriage. I felt the faceless men's presence bleed into me even if I could not see them. The ponies were uneasy. I sensed their latent panic: as if something stalked them.

It was not natural. None of it was right...

Solancei

Just Fatigued

"Princess Iambre! My Lady!?"

As from another world, Palea al'Duchino's voice mingled with Ina Uttorian's, reaching beneath the thick landslide of mud that buried Iambre. For a few long beats, she did not recognise her own name but the clamouring hands and high-pitched calls would not desist.

She murmured for them to be quiet but the communiqué was but a groan.

A small commotion erupted. She imagined more than felt the disturbance in the air as the two handmaidens were suddenly by her side. Esardan melody, she recognised Ina talking in a rapid torrent of insistent instructions and she wondered groggily if the words were meant for her. *Comprehension failed. Her eyes did not seem to work. She was in a black space within herself. It was immense...*

"...must slow down!" She heard Ina say, the melody of her accent full of jarring concern. Sensing the woman's face a mere inch from hers, she stirred with another groan. Bewildered by the idea of Ina' distress, the dark space receded.

"Princess, you must breathe slowly! My Lady! My Lady listen!"

Iambre peeled her eyelids apart with effort. Her chest felt heavy, her body too tired for words. Through a haze she saw Ina's unlined features creased in a wealth of anxiety, a filigree pattern of worry now rendering the still-young handmaiden older by twice her years. *Iambre didn't understand...*

Disappearing briefly from her limited line of view, Ina reappeared with a small stone vial in one hand and a dipper in the other. Iambre blinked, the smell emitted from the pot, both quickening and sweet. From the left, she heard Palea squeak something in question, but

130

Ina's head clipped in denial. Then she was swimming in a smell so arid that for a moment she truly could not breathe at all.

Iambre coughed, her breath retching, scratching through chest and throat, leaving the soft tissue within raw. Jolting, she issued a sound of disgust and denial, the frost-laced breath rushing in and out her lungs without mercy now, slashing holes through the darkness and banishing the heavy load from within her body.

Another painful breath, and another; on the fourth, the darkness vanished, bringing her back to the floor of her bedchamber in a crumbled heap of skirts and skewered hair. A twin pair of eyes, corners furrowed in concern, peered down on her: the two ladies normally so different, now wearing near-identical expressions as they knelt on either side of her.

The Princess groaned under her breath, equally embarrassed and thankful. Staring up at the fabled animals painted amongst the ribbons of red and green on the fantastically decorated ceiling, Iambre tried to rediscover her aplomb.

"Your Grace, thank Gods!" Palea exclaimed, fawning with pleasure.

Iambre smiled weakly. *She was on the floor. On the floor...*

With a cleansing gasp, she issued a shaky breath and a tiny, unsure peel of self-conscious laughter that failed to convince anyone as she weakly pushed at the two women to sit up without the aid of their good-will attention.

"My... thank you, ladies." Iambre rubbed her chest, still feeling the sting of the smelly salts in the back of her nose and throat, although Ina had passed the jar back to Palea who was now placing it back into Iambre's small arsenal of medical remedies at the foot of her bed.

131

"My Lady... are you stable?" Ina's concern was palatable as she felt Iambre's forehead and then her pulse.

"I... I don't know... I don't know what happened." Feeling silly, Iambre shifted her eyes to encompass them both. *Last time this had happened, in lieu of 'morning glory', Lancei had slapped her so hard she'd left a red handprint...*

"Please... could you?" Iambre gestured vaguely to the chair and Palea hurried to her side to help Ina as the older handmaiden moved to restore the Princess to her former seat.

"Highness, I am so sorry." As though she was personally to blame, Palea kneeled before her, the picture of chagrin. Wringing her hands she said, "I thought... I thought I would only be a quarter of an hour but then the Knights Commander called me back for a word in confidence, and I..."

"Palea, this is not your fault," Iambre reassured the girl tiredly, her mind too messed up to care for Palea's words about Zulavi, though she knew she ought to ask. *Later...*

"My Lady had I but known I would not have left you." Ina now. *Looking anxious. Not for herself but for what might have been...*

Iambre issued a short laugh. "Believe me Ina: had I but known too, I would not have dismissed you."

Ina's pallid smile made Iambre ashamed for the semi-harsh dismissal earlier. It was a little thing but she put a hand on the other woman's arm. In line with a gentle squeeze, she said, "I am only glad you decided to come back. Thank you both again. I don't know what came over me."

Ina padded the hand on her sleeve. "Fatigue, Your Grace. No doubt nothing but fatigue. Now let us get you ready for bed and-"

"No Ina, you have done enough for one day." Iambre squeezed her arm again. "You go to bed now. Tomorrow will be yet another long day. Get some rest."

Ina gave her a long look, then acquiesced with a small curtsy. "As my Lady commands, but I am only just next door, don't forget!"

The two women watched Ina leave in silence, then Palea drew herself to her feet, smoothing the crumbled taffeta panel of her top skirt. In the wake of her loss of control, Iambre swallowed bile; she did not know why she got like that. It had happened a lot when she'd been adolescent. Her mother had told her to pucker up; that she'd grow out of these attacks and that they were not life-threatening. As she recalled, her parents had shared livid disagreements about Iambre's supposed affliction, her father insisting that she'd be supervised by a medic at all times and her mother telling him that this was yet another reason why the realm seemed to flounder without direction: his inability to let go of things! Iambre had not seen the relevance, but usually she never did when her parents argued. It seemed to start out as one thing and end as another: a thing she could all too easily relate to when she and Lancei had their spats. *What was a question about the interpretation of a stupid old text, would turn into a thing about a hairbrush, or a page boy, or a fight over which outfit should be worn at Iambre's next engagement.*

"Just do my hair quickly now, Palea. You need to rest too." Iambre looked at her young handmaiden with a wan smile. She could easily undo the tightly plaited coiffure herself but she did not want to be alone right then. *Her chest still felt tight...*

133

Iambre coughed, earning her a concerned look in the mirror from Palea's deep-blue gaze and in a beat the girl's already big round eyes seemed to grow even wider.

"Daisies and dandelions, My Lady, but you're ashen!" the girl exclaimed, her busy fingers leaving off the intricate knots of the ribbons in favour of preparing the Princess a fresh cup of tea.

Iambre clasped the offered beverage with shaking hands and Palea's soft mien hardened like a troubled senator's. "Respectfully. If Her Highness is sick, then I must get Lady Riselta. Ina said no, but now I..."

Palea searched Iambre's face in the mirror, undoubtedly hoping to catch a glimpse of her true feelings, but Iambre only nodded her chin 'no' and swallowed a deep mouthful of tea. *She felt dizzy but she was not about to tell Palea.*

"I am just fatigued. That's all," she whispered. "Perhaps there is something about that headache after all. I do not seem to be myself. Please, sort the ribbons and leave the plaits, I think I need to sleep."

"Ah but of course." Palea nodded, licking her pale lips just once before setting back to her job at Iambre's hair with a vigour and dexterity of fingers that proved just how much she feared her mistress about to fall off the 'perch'. By the look in her eyes, Iambre could tell that the girl desperately wanted to fetch wise-woman Riselta, and yet she daren't usurp the Princess' instruction.

Iambre smiled softly to steady the young girl. *Her mother had not approved of Palea joining her retinue either, she recalled. 'Too young!' Ishjah had argued. 'She will not know how to cope.'*

Iambre swallowed the warm beverage and savoured the infusion of herbs and honey as they went down. *Perhaps her mother had been right? Palea had a nervous disposition but then again... which* eighteen-winters old who'd been locked away from life in a temple since the age of ten would not feel that way?

Iambre wiped the unpleasant idea from mind before it could colour her expression. Even when they were miles removed from each other, her mother still had the ability to ruin her peace. *Death and daffodils!*

Feeling the twisted weaves uncoil, followed by a few dozen smaller ones, Iambre looked up. Her skull itched: a sure sign that it would soon hurt too, which meant that she'd worn her hair too tight for too long. If she went to bed like this she'd awaken in half an hour, thoroughly uncomfortable and in need to undo the finer plaits.

She drew a deep breath through her nose and found Palea's round eyes.

"I cannot sleep like this," was all she said.

"I thought it so My Lady." Palea agreed without drama and carried on loosening the additional strands, religiously running the bone comb through each skein as she went.

There was something therapeutic about the handmaiden's rhythm and the hands filing through her hair; in the mirror, Iambre saw her own pallor recede before a starburst of rose across each prominent cheekbone.

You cannot go around exploding into these sort of panic attacks every time things get a little problematic, she scolded herself, *it has to stop! I am to be Queen! Things will be right! Just as they are supposed to be! They have to be! And Bilan will cease to matter; Solancei will be back and Tuxama will be grand! There!*

And almost she believed her own lies, when in truth she did not really want Bilan not to matter, nor go to Tuxama, nor be Queen, or-

Not be Queen?

135

For a blink, Iambre forgot to breathe again, this time not because of panic, but because of the sudden self-awareness as truth slapped her squarely in the face.

She did not want to be Queen! Mercy...she did not!

Iambre swallowed hard desperation.

With insight she seemed to have previously lacked, she realised also that Lancei had seen this coming for over a year, maybe more. *Bilan was not the reason but he had been the catalyst and now he was very much a reason! Gods...*

Still staring into the mirror as Palea released a waterfall of hair over her face to work at the final weaves, she wondered what her mother would say to this? *What Bilan would say?*

'Nothing, you fool!' a voice seemed to thunder in her mind, 'They would say nothing because you can never tell them! Never!'

Iambre felt herself run hot then cold. *You have to be the Heiress! Have to! And you know this! There is no one else!* She had other cousins besides Lancei, of course. Yet not one of them could step into her place without dire repercussions! And the realm counted, she chided. This was not just something that could be thrown away or brushed aside! The realm would never disappear; there would never be anything else for her than this... *her 'blessed inheritance'...* because this was what she'd been born to do. Bilan saw this too and bless him... *bless him...*

Iambre let her tired head sink back into Palea's hands as the handmaiden finished, gathering up the long wavy curls and giving them just one final brush before plaiting the mass into one simple braid for the night. *It felt like she'd just had an epiphany, only to lose it behind a mountain of clouded thoughts, never to be seen again. Gods!*

Bottom lip quivering, though with what emotion she no longer knew, Iambre steadied her nerves only through habit. Soon Solancei would be back, she reminded herself! *And, that was good! Yes! And, something to cling to!*

"Nothing else matters than the Realm and the Unified Provinces", she repeated aloud to herself for the benefit of her fleeing sanity. *Nothing but the Realm...*

"My Lady?" Palea enquired, raising her gaze, but Iambre dismissed her with a shake of her head

Whether she wanted to be Queen or not, did not matter. She had no choice... *and against all of this, how could she ever have persuaded Bilan to stay? Somehow he saw everything so much clearer; had done since the beginning...*

Iambre sighed but it was covered by Palea's, "There My Lady."

Eyes sting though they remained strangely dry, she managed a wooden nod of thanks. *This was too big for her to cope alone. She needed Lancei back! Gods, she needed her friend back! And soon! Only Lancei would understand! Only Lancei, and no one else, could help see her on the straight and narrow right through to Tuxama. Without her friend...*

Without her, I am lost. Iambre curled her fingers into balls and stood up, her cotton under-dress swaying around her legs. *Lancei had loved and lost and so would she!* They'd be like sisters of a secret order, she decided with a certain smattering of caustic cynicism. Like comrades of a battle fought and lost...

'It was better to have loved and lost than never to have loved at all!' That's what 'they' said, wasn't it?

She felt her face twitch with distaste. To her, the stupid maxim seemed nothing but midnight raffle and she had a feeling that if she

137

ever were to ask Solancei for her outright opinion, her friend would 'laugh' out loud at this naivety too. *Love lost... hah, it was ludicr-*

"My Lady? Will you want me to help you into your nightwear?" Palea interrupted, bringing her mind back to focus. Iambre started saying 'no', then halted on half an 'o' as she looked at Palea's face.

Now that she'd managed to alleviate the young woman's worries in regards to her health, Iambre suddenly noted something she hadn't previously and in spite everything it peaked her interest. It was not like her to miss these things, but the veiled aura of excitement that seemed to hover around the handmaiden was suddenly unmistakable.

Iambre cocked her head in question. *It was almost a relief to centre her mind on someone else - perhaps even selfish refuge - but-*

"You seem in better spirits," she commented with a small upturned lilt to the final syllable.

"Why My Lady, it's... it's just that I am very pleased you are not ill. It... it had me gravely worried to come back and find you... thus." Palea looked down, eyes floating away from the Princess in what could only be described as 'curious evasion'.

"Well, maybe you should stay and help me?" Iambre strolled casually to her bed where some local chambermaid must have turned down the covers and left a sprig of lavender. Something was twitching in the back of her mind. *Something Palea had said about being late...*

Sitting down on the bed, Iambre padded the cover next to her. "Come sit for a while. You seem uncommonly excited? Let's talk. Is there something I should know?"

Palea wrung her hands and looked anywhere but Iambre as she flushed puce to match the painted ceiling ribbons. It left Iambre swallowing surprise. She'd seen Palea flush before: it was a regular feature: the girl was Zanzierian-pale, but this...?

"Well?" Iambre pushed, taken with intrigue, perhaps more pleased than the situation warranted to have something mundane to suppress her own thoughts when they seemed to bring only sadness and regret.

"Well?" she repeated with a lilt of intrigue.

Palea looked up, catching her eye, then flushed scarlet again. As if in disbelief of her own capitulation, the girl shook her head; upon a deep breath, she finally said, "I... I cannot describe the feeling. Something... something has happened to me and... and..."

Seemingly lost for words, Palea smoothed her suddenly shaking hands down the front of her skirt, as she came and sat next to Iambre. The high colour was leaving her face a little, rendering it rosy instead of red, but her air of excitement only seemed to be growing as she fiddled with the charms on her ornamental belt, making little sounds as she tried to speak, then discarded what she'd been about to say.

The Princess had never known the young woman so tongue-tied, but the slightly dreamy look in her eye could only mean-

Iambre's suspicions flared. *No! No surely not?*

Iambre sat back. Semi-shocked.

"I... I did not mean for this to happen," Palea apologised, noticing Iambre's scrutiny and looking doubly interested in a small eagle dangling off her belt. The young woman appeared to be blushing all over just looking at it and Iambre knew then that she was right. *Her eighteen winters old handmaiden was in love!*

139

For a moment, Iambre remained too stunned to think. Had she really been so blind that she'd missed this? Or was this a brand new thing?

A half-hearted semi-genuine smile sped across her lips, pulling her mouth upwards, though only for a blink as uncertainty rode in to spill doubt. *She should have known about this! Gods!*

Striving to fit her face and sentiment into the expected frame, Iambre pressed her mouth into a tight line, refusing to speak first and allowing Palea the space to build up courage to explain herself. It took absurdly long, but then...

"My Lady, I could not help it... I mean who can?" The young woman caught her Mistress' gaze, a secretive smile that Iambre had never before seen, now playing on her rosebud lips.

It was disturbing on a foreign level when the handmaiden said, "These things just happen, don't they? Like they sing about: it just happens? As it were, he'd been watching me all night. I saw him look at me: over and over, and..."

Palea cut off, suppressed a shiver and made a gushing sound of pleasure as though she was elsewhere far more intimate.

"But... but how?" Iambre knew she sounded too shocked, but... *Gods, it barely seemed possible.*

Palea simpered. And then, as though once more unable to contain her own thrill from spilling over, the handmaiden flung her hands down and bounced her seat against the bed as she finally looked directly at Iambre. Smile widening to show her small, nearly-perfect teeth, she exclaimed, "Oh, My Lady, I wanted to tell no one, but knew I could not contain this from you for long. Now do tell me you agree: is he not just famously handsome and intriguingly unconventional? Tell me, is he not?"

140

Gods be good! Iambre's eyebrows shot towards her hairline in mock question. There was something she did not like about Palea's outburst, something alarming.

As pleasant as it had felt moments ago to concern herself with this small trivia, it was a sudden fight to battle down the uncanny suspicions now vibrating within. For some reason, she had the most disturbing idea that she already knew exactly 'who' Palea was talking about - and unfortunately it killed her joy of intrigue and what spark of pleasure she might have felt to share this moment with her young friend.

"Why my dear Palea," she managed, "I... I do believe you are...? Are... in love?"

Palea grinned and just like that, the knot in Iambre's belly bunched again but she looked back at the handmaiden with a frozen smile, hoping against all odds that her assumption was about to be proven wrong.

"So do tell me..." Iambre paused, an urge to shy away from the question, gnawing deeper. With lips that seemed too stiff to bend into words, she carried on, "So who is this fortunate man, I wonder? Would you... tell?"

Ignoring Iambre's question Palea simpered, her next words falling fast and low, as if talking to a conspirator of sorts, "Oh My Lady, I shall not bear it till I see him again. How do people do this? Gods, but I must confess to you that I now recognize the fire in me that Ina and the older ladies would sometimes talk about in much detail. It is... wondrous!"

Iambre regarded her with a slightly acerbic smile. "Wondrous? Hmm yes, I suppose, but dear girl, surely no one should-"

"Oh, I am so sorry..." Palea interrupted, now at ease with the intimacy of their setting and lost to her own, as she said, "I mean no slight, but... well, I am sorry, but... but if My Lady has never had such feelings for anyone, you will of course not be able to understand. Goodness how silly of me! Well, your Grace, let me confide even if you could not understand, that from now on I shall simply walk amongst the clouds!"

Iambre watched the girl look at something only she could see and felt a sliver of nuisance come over her. *The girl was daft! Did she think herself the only one to ever fall for a smouldering stare and a set of wide shoulders? Pah!*

"My dear Palea..." She tried again, careful to seem only curious, "You simply cannot keep me in suspense like this. I am your Mistress and I demand that you tell me the name of this man who has so managed to befuddle your senses."

Startling slightly, Palea paused for a blink, clearly not quite able to puzzle out if Iambre had just paid her a slight insult. Then she said, "My Lady... I must protest. I am not befuddled."

"Oh...?" Iambre manipulated her voice to mirror apology, "Well then I must just misunderstand."

Palea hesitated, then relented with a small peal of delight, "Oh well all right, My Lady, I will tell you. First, however, I will have to swear you to secrecy."

"Fine. Swear me to secrecy, then." Iambre felt her nuisance return. "Gods Palea, anyone would think you'd fallen for the King Himself!"

"Nearly." The girl smiled widely, once again the conspirator. "Although, begging your pardon My Lady, the King is not exactly... you know... young."

Iambre stared, her mouth hanging open. Belatedly she gathered herself.

"Just tell me the name of this mysterious man," she told the girl flatly.

"Oh My Lady, I tease you but have you not already guessed?" For a blink, Palea's large eyes turned even larger as she stared into Iambre's. Then she blurted, "My Lady... surely...? Well, surely you would admit that the Knights Commander has caught your eye as well? I mean, how could he not? He is so dashing, and tall, and when he speaks, everyone listens."

Palea sat back, her eyes sparkling in the light of the bedside lanterns. Iambre, meanwhile, slowly tried to assemble an appropriate answer, but words escaped her. *The Knights Commander... just as she'd feared. Funny, but she'd never before thought Palea blind, or dumb, or even plain stupid, but with a few words...*

Stomach bunching, Iambre opened her mouth to comment but once more unable to contain herself, Palea overruled her, "And so handsome too, is he not? With eyes the colour of blue diamonds - just like the set your mother gave you, don't you agree My Lady? My... when he looks at me I cannot think. And he's powerful too: near enough to rival your own good father - begging your pardon and no offence, that is."

"None taken, my dear," Iambre muttered. The swag of her plaited hair had fallen lose over her shoulder to obscure part of her face and it conveniently served to hide her belaboured expression. Of course, it could not hide her keen note of dry sarcasm in quite the same way, but Iambre doubted if Palea even heard, for she simply tittered and proceeded to spin out yet more words of praise for Zulavi.

Iambre only listened with half an ear. *So Zulavi was making eyes at her youngest lady in waiting? What the fleck did he think he was doing? Finding yet another way to stir offence?*

Her gaze swivelled to the small but heavy chest that housed her jewellery and such. The diadem set in question was of course beautiful, but she hated the way Zulavi appeared to study her when he thought her unaware: with eyes the colour of-

Disliking the new connotations in her mind, on a whim and half-a-thought she wondered if the set might be broken down as presents for the dozen new handmaidens awaiting her in Tuxama? She saw the jewels in her mind very clearly and Palea was right: the man had eyes the shade of blue diamonds: sparkling cold and as void of feeling as they were of colour. Thus far, however, rather than priceless gems, those eyes had reminded Iambre of a snake's, yet now...

Though meant in a different spirit from Iambre's, Palea's analogy lingered. Iambre had always loved the pale diamonds, but now? With this new association?

Annoyed that she'd had the thought, Iambre waved it away. The problem of unwanted jewellery was for later; for now, she had more pressing matters on her mind. *Palea's infatuation shocked her!* Gods be good, but in the space of one day, the girl had gone from finding the Zanzierian as tedious as the Esardan were unconventional, to suddenly swooning over their Head of Province as if he was a picking saint returned from the Void. If that was not a mad change of heart and wrong to boot, she didn't deserve to call herself 'Princess'!

Palea was of course old enough to run her own house, but she might as well have been but thirteen for all of her blue-eyed innocence. It didn't mean she wouldn't prove bold enough to do something stupid though. *People in love did that,* she reflected.

She quenched a sigh. Zulavi had made an impression on her young handmaiden, but perhaps it was to be expected? The 'girl' had been Zulari'Chi's servant for nearly half her life; Iambre knew no other man of wealth and standing had ever looked twice before - because the deity of Wisdom and Knowledge was as jealous as any God of His acolytes. *He* would not have tolerated another suitor for His attention, except perhaps the Princess of Ostravah herself when she came a-bearing gifts worth a year's taxes.

Iambre felt a stab of protective care roll through her. The way she saw it, she'd come to Imkarah looking for a scribe and had rescued a lonely girl in the same breath. *Now she'd be damned if she let Zulavi turn the girl from her more valued duty when she'd finally begun to settle! Was Zulavi thinking he could have a little fun, then turn Palea out? Did he think her that innocently stupid - or was it some other motive driving the man?*

Iambre didn't care. *This one, he'd better lay off!*

Solancei's Memoirs

The Province of Tarléon.
Hilt's pass; westbound.
Autumn of 780 P. C. W.

As my parents' coach drew onwards to straighten once more, I believe this was the moment when I first became aware of... of the stench of something 'other'. It almost felt sentient - not a word I knew then - but it trailed like Arbar'Chi's cracked nails along the insides of my head: the sensation raised was one that might have felt like the beginnings of a migraine, but there was a dark vivacity behind it. It both repelled and fascinated: it was something I wanted to both examine the intricate layers of and at the same time cower from. *It made me shiver violently as it drew my awareness further outward - and in that blink, I truly sensed the night-time hour not the reason for the lacking flow of conversation between the adults!*

My feelings thickened as something seemed to reach for me across the ice, and snow, and wood, and metal, and cloth of everything that surrounded me. Fear swept through me: consuming; twisting; exhausting. Where the peace previously offered by the State of Veranto had gone, I didn't know - it somehow did not exist in this place - but my heart had begun to canter: the idea of something 'wrong' no longer a feeling that I could suppress as it spread like an invisible mist within our tiny enclosure, brewing like a poison rising off an alchemist's kettle to further pollute the already sombre atmosphere.

A sound that was not a sound registered. It might have been in my head; it might have been outside, but my nausea came back, intensifying, and my father's features clouded over with cold sweat just as we all then heard a vicious snarl trailing the carriage. My first thought was of Osari'Chi's Pale Sa'brans: that the wight-like creatures had stolen from the God of Chaos' ranks to come harvesting what they could from the living; of the living. *But the Sa'brans did not make sounds like the grating snarling hatred that seemed to float on the air as though it belonged to a creature that might be*

146

miles away one heartbeat, only to seem right next to the coach moments later. Sa'brans moved silently, without sound; in all its chilling promise, there was a layered quality to what I was hearing - a whisper on the edge of reason; a knowledge of the end.

It left my spine cold and hard like an icicle, but I knew it could snap with the right sudden pressure and it was melting: all the chilling water bleeding into the rest of me, soaking my insides, making me soft and diminished. My father's aide trembled just once, his narrow frame losing a little of its stiff-backed determination as he couldn't quite keep the shadow of ripening fear from his eyes; father's face, already pinched, lost the final edge of the lingering permanent anger he normally covered so well with a blustery attitude and affable words, and I pressed myself back against the old russet suede of my seat, wanting to reach for Taliana's hand but finding that I could not move. I gnawed on my bottom lip instead, and I swear I tasted blood, but then my mother sobbed just once: a huge sound that could have been exchanged for mirth but for the terror rolling off her elegant, fur-wrapped body, and I forgot about everything else then.

Another sound of something from another world registered with everyone then - a low whirring with a cadence of menace to be feared and my mother went rigid, her wide lips splitting on a sound that never made it through her mouth as she clasped Taliana's hand. I was almost jealous of her boldness; of her ability to move; of her ability to touch Taliana....

With mother's touch, my steadfast nurse looked grim, the crease separating her wide eyebrows further than ever the only clear sign of her worry, but I swear I felt the two women's knowledge of their imminent demise breathe into me then. For mercy, to this day I am convinced that they both knew there'd be no getting home from this, and in their own individual ways, both women were terrified as they clung to their seats and each other for faith and support.

The carriage jolted then righted. The whip cracked with relentless need now and the horses seemed to pull forth new power and speed then, the vehicle surging ahead as if given a gentle push from behind.

147

But the sounds of that which followed on our wheels might have been a little closer already, and I shall never forget it, yet still I cannot describe the essence of what I heard because it was too foreign, but of course I did recognise that very same sound years later when once again circumstances had pushed me into a corner - but that's both in the past as well as for later now, and not part of this event.

Still, I felt what the people in the carriage felt: it was bleeding into me like a lotion of sweet despair absorbed through the skin. Already it had immobilised me with something I imagined might have been real terror, because I did not recognise the deep emotional response in me, but I would certainly remember it too-well just the same.

Slowly expanding, it slinked deeper into me though: mingling with a now-realised musty feeling of poorly-restrained panic that vibrated like a sourly-scented aura off the adults in the cab. *It all felt wrong. Very, very wrong! My father's left hand was anchored to the plain wire hilt of his foot-long dagger now, his jaw clenching and unclenching, whilst his valet kissed a locket of gold, muttering prayers to Ulvaro'Cha, Goddess of Fear and Courage, although I could hear no word coming from his mouth.*

It made my eyes quest to Taliana again, but nothing was asked; nothing clarified. I might have queried this oddity too, but avoiding some obstacle, the driver chose that blink to pull-up the team of bays sharply, hence upsetting the flow of pace to send them into a series of stomach-turning manoeuvres that made the coach bounce and wobble before the four horses managed to straighten and rebalance their bulk to thunder onwards. *How did I know they were the four bays? Gods, but I didn't - yet I had a strange overview of the entire situation: I knew the exact stretch of road we were on, and how it narrowed some hundred yards ahead before turning; I knew the coach driver was sweating though the wind carried a chill factor to herald winter on the way; I sensed he feared the mad pace, made perhaps more poignant to me because of his understanding that there was no choice in the matter; I was aware of the escorting soldiers breaking off two and two, grey cavalry sabres already drawn, their eyes wide so to see*

148

better in the russet twilight that seemed to retain more colour than the leather at my back; the road was rising - I could feel the gradient - and sapient insight made me quiver as I knew what was coming.

Soon...

Soon we'd all be dead.

Solancei

Sweet Chatter, Rotten Concepts

Iambre clenched her fists, the half-moons of her nails leaving pink imprints on the insides of her palms. For a blink, she imagined the rambunctious Ina a few years younger, and for the first time wondered if it were a man like Zulavi who had first ruined her? *It might well have been.*

Ina was cut of a different mould, however, and she had turned the disadvantage to her advantage. Palea would not. Zulavi would eat her heart and spit her out - Iambre had no doubt whatsoever - and then Palea would be ruined; perhaps irreversibly, and without the personal wealth afforded her Patrician counterpart...?

Mood flexing, the Princess pictured Zulavi. Propriety ought to stop the man from dallying with one of the royal handmaidens, but Iambre was not stupid. Ina had told her stories; stories of 'things' happening behind curtains and closed doors; things that one might usually see through fingers with! *Had Zulavi set his sight on easy prey, then he would not let the small nuisance of Palea's affiliations stop him.*

"Palea..." Iambre smiled and swivelled on the bed so that she could clasp the handmaiden by the shoulders in a show of affection. Catching those big, questioning eyes, Iambre held her gaze and said, "Palea you are very dear to me, yes? Dear to me and dear to everyone in my entourage. Love... love is a wondrous thing indeed, but... but you must promise me to have a care, yes?"

Searching those wide eyes, Iambre squeezed her shoulders, giving her a small nod. *Understand?*

"But... but of course," Palea assured her, the timbre of her voice uncertain to match the slant of her mouth. "Please, My Lady, I would never act in a manner that would reflect badly on your good name; I would never-"

"No of course not." Iambre injected, gently stopping the girl's urgent assurances. Her confusion made her look as vulnerable as a lost doe and Iambre cursed the Gods. *Commander Zulavi most certainly had a good eye, for Palea was undeniably pretty.* Fragile sure, and ethereal almost - and yes, those blue eyes might seem just a little too large in her petite face but it was hardly a flaw! Any fool could see the woman swathed behind the flimsy fabric that constituted for a veil these days - and no one with eyes could miss the fact that Palea was too pretty for her own good. *Damn the man! Why did he not pick on someone his own 'size'? Like Ina...*

"My Lady is displeased and I humbly apologise." Palea al'Duchino had lost a bit of her glow now, and instead of an excited conspirator, she sounded anxious. Iambre regarded her, wondering if she'd let too much show on her face. *She was usually better than that, but...*

"Please," the girl carried on, voice mousy, "my remark about the King was not intended to be a slight or in any way discourteous. Please, Highness, you must know this!"

"Oh?" Iambre exclaimed; puzzled, but then understanding, "Oh! Yes! Yes, of course! That's fine Palea. Worry not. I realise this! Of course, I do. We are friends are we not? If it was a tad inappropriate to compare my father and Commander Zulavi, then I shall put it down to nothing more than flighty carelessness, wrought out of excitement."

Iambre smiled softly, feeling less forgiving than her words implied but knowing that she'd gain nothing by reprimanding her fuzzy-headed handmaiden.

"Thank you Highness, I have… I forget myself and have much to learn," Palea drew a steadying breath. "You honour me with your kindness repeatedly, even when I do not deserve it - but for you, I would've still have been in Imkarah, copying the old scrolls of Truth and sweeping the temple floors, but to my utmost surprise you chose me and-"

"Lady Palea, I will not have you belittle yourself before me or anyone else," Iambre chided, hoping to stop the young woman before she humbled herself too far. "You are born a noble, are you not? You are of a good family and from a long line of stout royal supporters, are you not?

"Anyway, regardless of anything else, you are now one of my ladies, a thing that gives you further status and standing, and I will not hear one of my closest speak as though she does not deserve her post. I chose you, remember? To believe yourself unworthy, you question my capability and my ability to make a sound choice, and that I certainly will not have. Understood?"

Palea shook her head in sheepish agreement. Subdued mien suffusing her face, she twisted fine fingers into the shimmering layers of the skirts pooling across her thighs, yet already that glow was returning to her eyes, and Iambre felt her spirits droop. *How to tell the girl in one breath, that she had to stand proud and think something of herself, only to inform her in the next that she'd never be 'good enough' for the Knights Commander and that she should forget this infatuation?*

To keep matters pleasant, Iambre allowed the girl to chat about the man, hoping to learn with a few well-placed questions, the actual extent of Palea's 'infection' - and how. It had the markings of an interrogation, but Palea was too green to recognize the signs and appeared to perk up at this 'pleasant exchange of gossip' between friends.

As it tallied, there wasn't much to second guess. The candles had barely burned a full notch before Iambre knew the ins and outs of the situation and to her dismay Palea's infatuation seemed to have been instant.

Cursing herself, Iambre did not know how she could have missed the signs of her handmaiden making cow-eyes at Zulavi, but apparently she had; the young woman apologised for this as well but Iambre waved it away. The damage was done. Gods, she herself was barely any better with Bilan, but again Palea surprised her. From the very moment of their twelve-hour belated arrival on the flagstones of Castle Zanzier's main yard, Palea had somehow managed to speak with the man a whole three times already, culminating in this less than casual conversation that appeared to have been the reason Palea had forgotten all about cold compressions and... well, her main duties!

If it wasn't for the ill feeling that seemed to stir in her belly whenever she thought about the Knights Commander, Iambre might have seen fit to at least applaud his efforts - not to mention Palea's - but as it were, she was too shocked. The man had a nerve; had put Palea in a compromising position when asking for her to rendezvous in a private reception room adjoining the main Hall. Then, once alone together, he'd proceeded to pry Palea with wine and had somehow persuaded her to remove the veil she should really have known better than to take off since it was a symbol of her standing; now thankfully he hadn't kissed her, but Palea nearly forgot to breathe as she turned carnation pink relaying just how close he'd come.

Alarm bells toiling, Iambre felt like punching something. "Did you agree to see him again?"

"No My Lady." Palea shook her head, managing a look of both prim relief and breathless disappointment. "And if you told me not to, I would decline a future offer too, although... although you should know that I felt perfectly safe in his presence. In fact, he asked about you too My Lady: about your preferences and whims, about your habits and tastes. Indeed, I think... I think he might have tried to learn if you would resist his attention to me and if so, maybe learn how to appease you, but... but... it all seemed to happen in a dream."

To Iambre, whatever the man was trying to do or not do, it hardly mattered. He'd had the audacity to detain one of her ladies, without specific permission no less - and by his actions, he'd assumed the right to treat Palea with far less dignity than had he come a-calling for her as would have been proper.

The knot in her stomach swirled slowly one-eighty. The ruddy man was 'testing the waters' for something, of that she felt sure. *Death and daffodils, and now Palea thought she was the luckiest girl alive.*

"And now you are in love?" Iambre stated, offering the handmaiden a candid stare, "My dear friend, are you ready to know such heartache, I wonder?"

Looking away, Palea padded a hand over her artfully twisted plaits though not a hair was out of place. It was a nervous gesture but one that the woman had started using to feign calm and gain a few moments to control herself.

With a serene face, she looked Iambre in the eye. "My Lady, I know I am only a lowborn nobleman's daughter, but...

"But I refuse to let the circumstances of my heritage closet my feelings. Nobility is more than a piece of parchment proclaiming your

154

title, so claims your help Solancei, and if she and I do not commonly see eye to eye, on this particular point I must find myself in agreement."

As the contents of the statement itself hit a soft spot within Iambre, it was overshadowed by Palea's poorly veiled jab at Solancei's position.

Iambre knew there was no love lost between Lancei and the other women but Palea's ability to lace her words with innuendo against Lancei was indeed another sign that she'd come far in adjusting to her new life; sadly, it also showed just how far she still had to go. *Help?*

Palea could not know, of course, that Solancei was so much more than just another *'help'*, but her assumption grated; as did the lack of respect.

"Palea," Iambre warned in a low voice, "I am uncommonly forgiving of personal dispositions, yet less so of thoughtless views. I beg you to have a care now for how you speak of my other handmaidens, or this time you will be too bold, you understand."

"My Lady." Palea sighed without a hint of rancour to be chastised and bobbed her chin prettily to acknowledge the reprimand. Too earnest, she said, "I apologise of course, but my point here is not about Solancei, but about shared views. Now, if I may be so bold? Solancei has ever told me that one must follow one's heart to be true to life and purpose. I didn't comprehend before now, but I can see that it is sound advice."

"She does...? You do...?" Iambre exclaimed, eyes widening to rival Palea's. Momentarily thrown, not only by Palea's ability to draw upon the supposed words of wisdom from the very person she'd just slighted, but also at the idea that Lancei should have given voice to

155

something so philosophical, she had to shake herself to return to the issues at hand.

"Palea my dear, Solancei says a lot of things but never mind! Tell me instead if Zulavi has given you direct reason to stand encouraged that he might offer you... more? If so, I would need to speak to him." *To warn him off...*

"My Lady, he has gone out of his way to speak to me, several times now," her handmaiden reflected, simpering again, "and though I do not have your learning in reading people, I see that he likes me very well."

Iambre smiled benignly, but her anger was back on a breath, scratching at the surface. In all likelihood, the Knights Commander saw well enough just what standing Palea had, but if his antiquated views should ever extend to the task of choosing a wife - *and indeed one not of Zanzier* - no matter what he had Palea fooled into thinking, the girl would never be the woman he'd consider for this questionable honour.

The slight play to Palea's conscience had been a cheap stab at staying the girl. It made Iambre feel like a hypocrite to speak of honour and short-selling when clearly she herself was already so ruefully guilty of disregarding both - but she told herself this was different. Standings might rise, yes - but Zulavi would certainly wish to marry someone of *Select Blood* - an ego like his would allow him nothing less, she felt sure.

I should tell the girl, she thought, yet held her tongue. One look for Palea's face told her of the futility. *The woman would not listen. Just like I would not listen, neither will she!*

Suppressing a sigh, Iambre reluctantly added this new problem to her rapidly-growing list. Thanks to Zulavi, she would now have to

156

watch her moon-brained handmaiden like a hawk for the remainder of this visit or else risk finding herself with yet another indelicate situation on her hands. *Gods defend... could her life get more complicated?*

"Palea, listen-" she began, then paused for a blink to search for the right words before she carried on, "-I think it wonderful if you are taken with a man, really I do! But my dear, do not mistake fascination with love - it's easily done, I'm told! Please see to it that you give yourself time to reflect on the verity of your feelings now before committing to anybody or anything. Someone of such high martial rank may not be the right match for you. Please... give it time to be certain. And for the love of every deity we know, please do not do anything rash or thoughtless - provoked or otherwise. Your honour is my honour, you will remember this, won't you?"

The earnest, open smile returning, Palea nodded. "My Lady, your council means much to me and I will think further upon your word. Still, I must tell you that should the Knights Commander indeed see fit to extend me an offer, then I fear I shall not be able to resist his charm. Please forgive me."

Forgive me? A shiver raced through Iambre, an invisible hand of finality carving an end to her willingness to speak further on the subject.

"Ach but My Lady, I could chatter the night away and you are not well!" Palea noted with a glance for the water clock. Belatedly aflutter like a mothering hen, she stirred into action. "Now let's get you a-bed or Ina will have words with me on the morrow. Black lines under the eyes are hard to cover."

The Princess nodded and bore up as the handmaiden fussed, applying brisk tones reminiscent of Lancei when her cousin boded no interruptions. Somewhat thankful that Solancei was not there after all, to add any of her usual drops of acid to the conversation, Iambre remained quiet as she stood to allow Palea space to help her shed the remaining few layers of daytime wear.

The handmaiden worked with a small frown on her forehead, and Iambre was relieved that the girl at least appeared to think on her words. *But Palea must be mad,* she reflected with a stab of confusion; *Zulavi was-*

The right words failing to materialise, she winched instead. After what Eso had told her about the jackal fight and Lancei, she could barely look the man in the eye without wondering what had truly happened and if he knew anything about Solancei. It would not help her one bit to go speculating where there were no facts to pave the way, of course, but now Palea thought the man 'charming' and fancied his attention? *It beggared belief!*

Iambre thought back years to the past then; to the time when she had first been introduced to a then-younger Knights Commander at her parents' court. Nothing much had changed, she mused, nothing at all. She hadn't liked his superior air or cold eyes then - and she still didn't! Fortunately, however, she'd had little to do with the man then and after their initial meeting, she could count their subsequent 'encounters' on one hand. *Until they'd been re-introduced at the tours in Keriko six years ago, that was...*

By then, Zulavi's youthful disdain had developed into a full-blown affliction of adult arrogance, and it had seemed to raise in her a new and almost instant adversity to his presence. Death and daffodils, and where many others might have fawned over the presence of a famous young knight at their side, she'd soon managed to invent a list of elegant excuses to avoid his company whenever it could not be politely excused. *Fawning? No not her!*

In fact, her unspoken dislike had touched so deeply, that for many a tournament, she'd actually preferred to offer the traditional 'ribbon of favour' to a string of her father's oldest champions rather than to Zulavi - an act most had considered very 'generous'.

Iambre's mouth quivered with a half-formed smile at the memory. To this day she still recalled being politely teased for her eccentricity, but it hadn't mattered. She had simply demurred and smiled, which in turn had earned her subsequent winks and the odd sly comment on her excellent political shrewdness. Iambre had never minded how her actions had been misconstrued for it had served as a good smokescreen - a better one certainly, than an admission of the truth that she simply hadn't wished to risk Simarovien Zulavi's extended attention. *It had been naive, of course, but it had worked; would that she could still play such games without discovery. Would that she could...*

A sigh escaped her. *Another one!* She might be a fool for Bilan and she might secretly adore the way he called her 'Milady' in that slanted accent of his - but at least he was a good man. *A good man,* who possessed a far more charismatic presence and unwavering sense of honour than the damn Knights Commander could ever hope to achieve in a lifetime! How her father had ever seen fit to promote Zulavi to his current status, she could only marvel at, for he had few refined manners and even less tact! *The idea of him and Palea? Well it infuriated, and if he knew anything of what had happened to Lancei...*

Biting her thumbnail, her unspoken worry for her wayward cousin flared back up for what seemed to be the hundredth time.

"My Lady, step through here, please," Palea urged and Iambre startled, then moved like a mechanical contraption as Palea directed. For some reason her mind rolled back to the 'uncomfortable' conversation she and Lancei had shared directly before they'd parted on Knight Laurelsday: a conversation where she had spoken to her friend in haughty demand and twisted warning; a conversation she now deeply regretted, along with all the others...

Gods, but what if she never saw her again? She had to tell her that she was finally ready to own up to her mad behaviour; had to tell her that she'd finally been brave enough to face the truth... and accept it.

Iambre swallowed hard to force down the same forsaken tears that kept returning and drew a deep, shuddering breath that had Palea look up in mild surprise. She pretended not to see and the handmaiden relieved her of the final shift without a word, swapping it for the various layers of loose fabric that constituted current fashion in nightdresses.

How could things have gone so splendidly wrong? And what assurances did she have that nothing else went awry? Ina's? Kira'Cha's? She hoped so!

Iambre blew out her cheeks, swiping her hair clear for Palea to fasten the ribbons at the shoulders. *Had Zulavi stayed away, tonight might have turned out most agreeable,* she reflected, *indeed it was not his tardiness she'd had grief with, but rather his presence. The man was just odd. How did Palea not see that?*

Iambre caught a glance of the other woman and herself in the full-length dress-mirror and had to force her mind from imagining Lancei's almond-shaped, kohl-rimmed eyes staring back at her instead of Palea's large, pale-lashed ones.

Observing Palea's serious face as she focused on her task, a new lump seemed to develop in Iambre's throat. It was neigh-on impossible to imagine this girl laughing without reserve or apology the way Lancei was want to do over some titbit of news or commentary that Iambre might make - only then to kill 'the royal wit' with one straight eyebrow raised to underscore some laconic or poignant observation or judgement. Gods be with her, but it had been too long since she'd given Lancei anything to laugh about and her guilty conscience seemed to float dangerously near the breaking point then.

"All ready now My Lady." Palea stepped back. "Do you require a draught to settle your humors?"

"No," Iambre declined, the prospects of bed slaying her final reserves. "I just need to relax now. Leave the clothes and go see to yourself now. Ina will attend me in the morning."

Nodding her dismissal, Iambre yawned, retreating into the rich softness of the heavy four-poster bed that had become hers for the duration of her stay.

A sigh of a better kind escaped her; the covers were thick Etruian linen and soft sable pelts – probably from Khelt – and the sheets bore the subtle fresh smell of dried herbs that made her thankful now for the third night in a row that someone had been thoughtful enough to ensure her a comfortable sleep.

Dousing candles and oil lamps, leaving just the one half-shuttered lantern on the bed-stand, Palea moved around the room like a silent shade only moments longer, then she bobbed a curtsy and withdrew silently to leave Iambre alone once more with her overwhelming array of thoughts. Tired though she was, her mind seemed unable to give her the quiet necessary for sleep and to pull free from the

161

quagmire in her head, the Princess tried to reflect on matters of little value: the large banquet hall, beautifully decorated, yesterday in blue and gold in honour of Knight Laurelsday, and tonight in red and gold to match the autumn theme of the menu.

It didn't work. Her mind had other plans; kept circling back and forth. *Palea and Zulavi... Gods, but how? There was nothing about the man to condone. Nothing.* Tonight he had not arrived at banquet before the serving of the fifth course. A fresh shaded mark on one cheek and a split lip made her wonder if he'd been fighting for sports to deliberately postpone his appointment, where after she had been able to think about little else but how not to respond to his ill-considered opinions and how to endure his obscene, frosty eyes without a shiver rattling her backbone whenever he looked her way.

Finally, she'd given up trying. Instead, she'd looked at him and wondered what he knew about Solancei? *She'd begrudged having to sit there 'the marionette'. Her cousin was still missing!*

To further spoil the unpleasant experience, throughout it all her anxiety had been gnawing at her peace of mind like a vial of corrosive poison inserted into her core until she seemed to have been made up of nothing but nervous looks and vacant requests for this or that question to be repeated.

Overall she supposed it sat well with her excuses to leave early, thank the Gods! For the second time she'd declined his escort, her best persuasive charm clearly not enough to assure him of the lacking need, yet the suggestion that he should not deprive his guests of company so soon after joining them, clearly another matter. Mercifully, he'd grudgingly agreed, thus thankfully sparing her a repeat of the previous night where he'd sought to dismiss Bilan's men. *And they'd refused.*

Iambre smiled in secret pleasure. Bilan was looking after her, even when he could not be there. Whatever he thought of the Knights Commander, he'd still taken on board her fears; had issued measures...

The Right of Command... hah! So simple and yet so binding. Refusing to null the Captain's command - feinting ignorant horror, yet using the premise that if her officer in charge had issued such orders, then who was she to interfere - her soldiers had stayed. Zulavi's face had been priceless, though - *livid under the colour sprang to mind* - but what did silly little her know of these things?

She only hoped Bilan would not get into trouble. This was Zulavi's house after all; she didn't want anything to befall the men and the Knights Commander had stood angered!

Thinking on it now, caused her to wonder if maybe that was the reason for his underhanded stab at seducing her handmaiden? *A kind of payback, to show her that he could ultimately command any of her people, where he wanted and when he wanted?*

It was not unlikely and the idea made her throat constrict.

Zulavi was proving unpredictable, but perhaps this was where she failed to understand him? *Perhaps,* she allowed, *perhaps this was his 'charm'; perhaps this was exactly what her father so valued about the man and perhaps it was exactly the thing what had made Zulavi a supposedly 'brilliant' military commander in the first place? Perhaps-*

Exhausted by her own snaking thoughts painting worries where none might exist, she shied from the notion of another night tarnished with verbal fencing and mindless smiles. *Gods but it had been a long day without Lancei; wondering, hoping, fearing.*

Frowning into the shadows, Iambre tried not to feel cornered. *Solancei would never leave. No matter what people said or thought, she just would not!* And besides, where would she even go? Ivanor would not be hers for another two years - if ever - and anyway, it would take her months to get there. Solancei had money and wealth - after a fashion - and could possibly make it far before she had to consider 'alternatives', but Eso had told her that nothing was missing from the chest of her Shield's belongings, and without money?

Lancei has no remaining family; no friends or distant relatives to take her in. *Why would she leave with nothing?* Iambre was her family; disagreements aside, was their relationship not as solid as that of true sisters'?

No, Lancei would never leave, but if she hadn't... If she hadn't...

Iambre's stomach churned, the now familiar vitrifying dread rising. *Why did she have the feeling that everything was about to change? Everything?!*

A Circle of Stones

"Be careful My Lord! What if-" Shock cut Lord Shuptah's warning short as the nine rocks deposited on the floor flashed into blinding light.

His aide's cowardly outburst would normally have inspired a cuff round the ear but this time Knights Commander Simarovien Zulavi was too pre-occupied to care. The Tuxaman 'loon' had briefed him and he had been expecting the flare, but the brightness was instant, and neither he nor Shuptah was fast enough to adequately shield their eyes from the paralysing glare as it hit the insides of his bedchamber with the purity of ten stars.

Taken aback, it froze Zulavi to the spot and for a good few debilitating blinks, he saw only an imprint of the leaves-upon-branches that withered across the cloth of his raffish gold coat when the flash-blaze played across the lustrous weave to reveal the handsome pattern with a shimmer of silk. Disturbed, thoughts pushed, threatening to unman him - *if someone attacked them just then, he'd be cut down before realising there'd been a need to defend himself!*

He strangled this useless weakness with a strength of discipline come from years of never letting himself sub-come to such dangerous lows. *Gods, but had the loon not told him that this was not a travelling, but a communications device? Even if he had only the word of a walnut to base such trust on, he doubted if an attack would be the first thing the Tuxaman was want to think of anyway!*

Zulavi forced the uncomfortable thought aside, blinking furiously, and catching a glimpse of his aide as the man cowered behind raised hands with a prissy look on his pasty-fine face that might have inspired an idea of entertainment at any other time.

Feeling instantly better, Zulavi grimaced. There was much to be said for this man his sister had sent him. *Sure, Shuptah would never be brave, nor even that smart, but he was dependable. Dependable and loyal.* And indeed, last night, was it not the aide who'd sent for the hedge wizard to apply healing to the sweet reminders that Angemar had left in evidence? And had it not been Shuptah who had also assured him of the need to take some time to wash and gain his aplomb before joining the Princess at the banquet?

As it were Zulavi was glad he'd listened to the weedy man. The royal lady had frowned enough at what remained after the hedge wizard's ministrations that she'd made him feel little better than some renegade street thug. The split lip still throbbed, but at least Angemar was gone, now. *One thing at a time.*

After the misbegotten banquet affair, Shuptah had been waiting too, as expected, where Zulavi had left him outside his chambers; the man had not as much as quibbled when ordered to fetch fresh wine, then make himself scarce again so that he might present himself at Zulavi's quarters bright and early before the hour of the red rooster, not long passed.

Yes, Shuptah had obliged as he did in most things! Indeed, this morning he'd not even argued when instructed to set the circle of stones as prescribed - although at this point the puny fool had begun shivering so badly with superstitious fright, that Simarovien had been forced to wonder if they'd have the set-up ready in time. *Seemed they had...*

He blinked again, but the light was rapidly losing its sting now. The Tuxaman walnut had likewise instructed that this would in all likelihood happen, but as it dwindled back in on itself, finally settling into a wilted, desiccated green that might have rivalled the colour of back-lit swamp water, the Knights Commander had to wonder if that was entirely right.

Annoyed with his own unease, he looked at the odd luminance, studying, making mental notes...

Magic. Who knew just what or how magic was supposed to behave? With the brilliance faded, new shadows claimed the recesses and corners of his room on a level that did not look quite natural: turning his coat a dull bronze now as the light flickered with less power than a flame behind the smudged lens of an ancient oil lamp. *Magic? The Tuxaman loon was surely a fool: there was no such thing as magic, and yet...*

From two paces to Zulavi's right his aide whimpered unintelligible words under his breath. *Gods!!*

"Shuptah, it's safe you dolt!" Zulavi spoke the harsh reprimand on a dry note of amusement, yet did not take his eyes from the now gently pulsing curtain of light that seemed to float like dreams, floor to ceiling, exactly where the nine strange stones rested upon the bare granite slaps at the centre of his chamber.

The glow retained a gossamer feel. *Like the veil of an exotic dancer.* Zulavi could see right through the wall of light to the other side where the large iron-bound chest - once his father's - sat against the gentle curve of the white-plastered tower wall, and he could just as easily pick out the assortment of heraldry and his selection of antique weaponry that had been hung directly above said chest on the very day he'd inherited Castle Zanzier in all its crumbling glory. It had been almost fifteen years ago now and since then he'd seen his share of interesting horrors - some of it created

167

by himself, some by the people in his employ - but he had never witnessed anything like this before. *Not even when face to face with the Tuxaman lord had he seen anything like this... this magic.*

Not sure how to feel, yet grudgingly forced to concede that whether magic or not, the Tuxaman nut had had a point in pursuing this wizardry, Zulavi cocked his head, for the premier time wondering if the man would be proven right on his other points as well. *Well, it remained to be seen - the loon seemed full of unusual surprises, but-*

"My Lord Commander, I see fireflies," Shuptah injected, belatedly lowering his arms to look directly at the dully green luminance.

Zulavi drew a deep breath.

"It will not last," he assured the aide, for a blink pondering why he'd bothered. Shuptah grunted but continued eying him askance whilst he blinked as though to clear his eyes of grit after being caught short by a dust-whirl on the training grounds *Presently, the aide looked thoroughly unconvinced that this was as it should be as well.*

"It's like a tainted river, is it not My Lord?" the aide mused then, smoothing back his neatly-oiled, well-trimmed hair with a long-fingered, slightly quivering hand, "like... like a clear forest beck that runs vertical in a world of myths and legends."

"Shuptah?" Zulavi didn't look away from the light but he was already feeling disenchanted with the promises the Tuxaman had made and perhaps it filtered into his tone, for the aide swivelled with a look of hope, perhaps thinking he was about to be dismissed.

"Yes, My Lord?"

"Be quiet!"

Shuptah made a sound as though he was swallowing his tongue but the Knights Commander couldn't bear the man's obsolete comments. Not now. *Gods, but this was not a natural thing to behold! It truly was not!* The curtain of vertical light seemed almost hypnotic as it did indeed ripple like the gentle waters of a vertical beck to cast a pattern of transparent waves across every surface of the room. It was all at once both compelling and unnerving, he thought. *Very unnerving; everything was still the same and yet...*

He hoped the loon would hurry up. He had matters to attend today, soldiers to brief, supplies to check, equipment and horses to move. Of course, he would not do this himself but a certain level of overseeing was required and it could not wait. Furthermore, he hoped to take a little time to check on the feisty trench he'd left in chains down below, feeling that she must have stewed for long enough now, that maybe...

Simarovien made himself look away from the light as though to prove himself able. The 'actual' natural light, produced by the three twelve-pronged candle stands stationed throughout the chamber, seemed van somehow - and yet there was something undeniably pleasant in the presence of the warmth they emitted. Gods, but he hadn't thought *this* would work-

No... correction: they hadn't thought it would work! And now...

In spite his own council, Simarovien quenched a shudder. *Magic? Now wasn't this a pip?* Well, whether it was or not, the fact remained that the Tuxaman Lord, Visentor Tan'Xaviar, had just proven that he might be more than a simple loon with a head full of strange ideas and a penchant for unsavoury experiments. *It might spell trouble. It might not. But as long as the other lord kept his nose in the books*

169

and his mind on feats of lunacy, then Zulavi was free to pursue his own goals.

Simarovien serenaded himself with a small nod. *If the loon insisted, who were he to prevent the other man from digging deeper into the recesses of the vermin-infested creases of those dusty old crypts that seemed to fascinate him so? Meanwhile, Zulavi himself would be busy above grounds - with the living. And the future.*

The Knights Commander stabbed Shuptah another glance from the corner of the eye. The aide looked as though he was staring into the Void. Again the man's expression harboured a hint of the comical as he swallowed almost painfully slow and absentmindedly rubbed both hands against the dark cloth of his breeches. Zulavi imagined Shuptah hoped to wipe away the memory of touching the stones, but then the aide seemed to gather some will, for he crossed both arms firmly across the Zanzierian emblem upon his chest and shot Simarovien a look of veiled admiration.

It made Zulavi's lips twitch, but before the other man could pick up something to say, the Knights Commander shifted sideways to study the phenomenon before them in more detail. Interestingly, though the reflection of the green light polluted his entire chamber, the gently ruffling boundary did not appear to spill out beyond the painted, smudgy-brown circle they'd made to connect the nine stones on his chamber floor. It must mean it was contained as expected and for the first time, he also noted that the contraption did not emit a single sound, either: not even the tiniest hum, nor buzz. *It was all just exactly as Tan'Xaviar had informed him. Every small thing. Every-*

"So who'd have thought, My Lord?" Shuptah ventured, voice more squeaky than usual and thereby capturing his Master's attention in less than a blink. "I mean, who'd have thought that a bit of thin blood and some old rocks could really do such an amazing thing? Hah - certainly not me! No sir, not me! Now I guess we just have to wait and see if our 'benefactor' can make this old parlour trick work the way he has been boasting. But probably not; I mean it is-."

"I already made it work you bleating imbecile!" a hollow voice intercepted, cutting through Shuptah's words with such a tone of contemptuous venom that Shuptah yelped with the wide-eyed alacrity of an unfortunate spirit hunter finally faced with the product of his investigations. As if the evil spirit was trying to touch him, he stumbled backwards till his backside met with the rectangular strength of a sturdy buttress.

This time Zulavi did smile. *Shuptah was an oaf but he might just make a convincing jester one day...*

The aide gave the Knights Commander a wide-eyed look of alarm, whispering, "Gods defend me! Gods forg-"

"Oh stop your blasphemy, fool!" the voice continued, carving an abrupt line through Shuptah's whimpering, "Lord Zulavi! Please remind your pesky little inferior to shut his mouth - or I will personally come through this circle and sow it shut with fresh-strung cat guts! Verity defend! So mark my words, I will!"

"Patrician Tan'Xaviar," Zulavi injected coolly, ignoring the threat, "please have enough courtesy to refrain from scaring my poor aide to death; it would be hard to explain the circumstances, I fear. Also, I believe my sister still fond of this brother-in-law, so maybe you... maybe you could oblige?"

Simarovien shrugged to himself even as he offered Shuptah a silent look of ripening contempt for the show of lacking restraint. It sent the aide's eyes briefly wide enough to reveal the white circling

171

each dark iris, and the man's brief googly-eyed status might have been the root of yet more amusement then, if it wasn't for the point that Zulavi pitied the man's inability to cover up neither mistake nor astonishment.

"Pah, but very well then." Tan'Xaviar's voice held a tired, droll note that wasn't disguised even with the slight distortion that seemed to mar the connection, ridding his tone of its usual soft power.

Simarovien gathered his faculties and turned his attention from the aide. He was aware that the other man seemed to sag as he exhaled but the Knights Commander left his impossible rancour behind. As expected, Shuptah didn't even pretend to hide relief as his near-sighted squint rolled up the decorative moulded ribbons of the chamber's architecture to the point where the half-rosettes flowed across the plastered, white-washed ceiling. *Well, as long as he did not faint...*

"Black rats, Commander Zulavi! Guess I should have known that you narrow-minded traditionalists would have reason to doubt my science," the incorporeal voice sang forth with scolding clarity and Zulavi braced himself.

Feet apart, jaw set, he crossed his arms, preparing to maintain the marrow-tight hold on himself that he was usually forced to adopt when it came to dealing with Lord Tan'Xaviar.

"But perhaps now you believe that my theories are not wholly founded on air and phantoms?" Visentor Tan'Xaviar continued, "Ah, no wait - don't bother: your answer is of course irrelevant!"

In the silence, the statement rang clear and seemed to settle like an oppressing mantle over the chamber's strained atmosphere. Zulavi clenched one hand into a fist - his only concession to the

172

slow-burning resentment he harboured towards the Tuxaman. *Tan'Xaviar might be an ally, but their alliance was not an easy pact.*

Zulavi frowned, striving to rise above petty argument. Anyone else calling him to question, he would have whipped for the offence, but Tan'Xaviar was old nobility, which often equalled few manners; the man had offered him the future so he could get away with much, but still...

Zulavi decided to bite down on the slight and let it pass. He could not afford to alienate Visentor Tan'Xaviar with pointless insults over intellect and abilities. The walnut would give him much and he'd have to recall just how important it was to the grander scheme. *Give the man a moment to gloat and then they would be back on track. He hoped.*

As expected, fortunately he did not have to wait long before Tan'Xaviar's incorporeal voice leaked back into the chamber.

"Oh come now, my dear fellows," the Tuxaman lord coaxed, the tone still hollow though it carried a slightly friendlier lilt than earlier, "your silence is touching, but I require no apology for the lack of faith you so clearly harboured for the workings of the Vidaria Stones! To have seen the look on your faces would've been priceless to me, but of course it does not work that way, so...

"Anyway, My Lords," he breezed on, "if you stand shamed by your lack of belief, then let the truth be your saviour, for you now know better."

Zulavi shifted his weight, trying to find a moment of peace. *He imagined the face belonging to that voice cracking with a self-satisfied smile just then, and he could almost see Tan'Xaviar's gloating strange eyes.*

173

"Well your words are gracious," he made himself reply with a slight twist of his mouth to show the extent of his real opinion, if only to Shuptah. After just the hint of delay, he added, "So the marvel of written words was rooted in truth after all. I am indeed pleased, My Lord. Very pleased, make no mistake Tan'Xaviar! And as for my 'aide'..."

He offered Shuptah a brief dismissive look. "Well, my Aide is ever a fool, so no offence taken."

"Well truthfully, My Lord Commander," the Tuxaman offered, very civilly now, "I'll freely admit that I expected no less of your tame oaf, but from a traditionalist like yourself, I suppose I expected a deeper faith in things rooted in the old ways. No matter though, it hardly pertains one way or another to this alliance of ours. Verily, let's move on."

Zulavi smirked to himself and sawed his teeth.

"Perhaps... that would be wise," he allowed, keeping the overall goal in mind: ever the Zanzierian hawk. *The Patrician lord was a loon, a walnut, but he would give Zulavi a chance to right the weaknesses that had slowly infested Ostravah, so yes by Osari'Chi, it was easy to overlook the other man's lacking grace.*

"So My Lord Tan'Xaviar is pleased with the result then? Pleased to find this... this contraption finally working?" Zulavi put on an agreeable voice to match the question.

"Artefact, not contraption!" the Tuxaman shot back, "And yes, one cannot help but feel excitement, however, the fact remains that there is still the pesky threat of my 'fiancée' looming on the near horizon and one wonders what you will do to rectify the situation?"

Zulavi allowed himself a fey smile. *He couldn't help himself...*

"Gods defend lord, you fear a small girl with a sunny smile and ribbons in her hair that much?" Zulavi poked at the other man's unease, the smile drawing wider. "Well, perhaps I shall do nothing; perhaps I shall take control of your small problem as agreed - but truly, the how and when will remain my decision and one best kept quiet for now."

"Lord Zulavi, we have an agreement," the other man warned, his strange, quiet voice quivering.

Pursing his lips, Simarovien Zulavi tutted. "Ah yes indeed we do. And how glad I am you still recall as much."

"My Lord Commander knows I do," came the man's sullen reply.

"Good. Then you would also recall that for this to succeed, I shall require your... *your special aid?*"

"I recall, but when? Time is growing short and I have work!" Tan'Xaviar sounded impatient.

The Knights Commander smiled thinly at the green veil as though the Tuxaman Lord might actually see him through the shimmering light, "And so have I Patrician; an army does not mobilise itself: now shall we discuss details as intended? I imagine you eager to learn the full extent of this artefact's power now that it has been restored to function. Tell me: where do you propose we start?"

"We start, my Lord Commander, with you confirming that everything happened exactly as I thought it would with the Vidaria Stones. Can you verify that the process remained true to description?"

"It appears to have activated in exactly the way you said," Zulavi allowed.

"Appears to or did do?" Tan'Xaviar questioned impertinently, "Which one is it now, My Lord? If the magic has not taken according

175

to the scroll's instructions, we may yet have cause for grief, so this is important now!"

Simarovien clenched his fists harder and saw Shuptah move imperceptibly at the other lord's choice tone. *By the hanged rat and bone, had the Patrician 'sap-head' not just boasted that he'd made the artefact work?*

Simarovien forced himself to recall that the walnut was not normal, then said, "Lord Tan'Xaviar, it worked exactly as you said - right down to this sickening algae-green light that seems to billow before my eyes like a spectre. Happy?"

"Yes, Lord Commander. Exceedingly." In the choice of tone, Zulavi could hear the other man calm down and allowed himself a curt smile of mockery over the ease with which one could turn Visentor Tan'Xaviar's mood around in a blink. Yet in a manner of speaking, he could relate to the Patrician though. Gods, but this was a fantastic thing, he allowed. After all, the loon was leagues away, in another province as it were, and yet they were 'conversing', free of parchment, couriers, or Red Wings.

"Now comes the moment of truth then, My Lord," Tan'Xaviar broke in, his peculiar tone laced with excitement now, "We shall enter into the circle past the threshold. Do you stand ready?"

Knowing what awaited him, and strangely fearing what else the moon-struck rich-boy might 'conjure up' in addition to all of this, Simarovien held back a moment longer, seeking to bank away any spare emotions. This was just *one thing* he reminded himself. *Just one thing! Gods but it might not even work!*

Afflicted by a burst of distrust, closely teamed with a keen sense of relinquishing control, Simarovien Zulavi had to remind himself that Tan'Xaviar needed him as much as he, in turn, relied upon the

Tuxaman. Their arrangements must count viable for a while longer and so in lieu of raising unnecessary conflict, Simarovien scowled at the ill-lit circle, trusting that whilst the man on the other side might be very talented, his scheming powers did not have the far reach currently envisaged. In any event, he'd have to take this to the end; one way or another, he needed Visentor Tan'Xaviar and if this was the required sacrifice then-

Simarovien glanced one last time towards Shuptah, looking for...? For what, he wondered. The uncertainty he felt at the idea of stepping across those stones and into that light was something he did not wish to dwell on, but at least he knew himself able to shield his own emotions better than Shuptah - something one had to be able to perfect if one did not want to offend the Tuxaman or worse!

Simarovien dismissed the aide from mind, turned towards the glow and smiled at the meandering veil with a predatory influx of patience. Tan'Xaviar might be the instigator behind this test, but none of this would've been possible without sad-old-mindless Angemar Cillario's involuntary collaboration from this end – something the nut had better remember. *Indeed, Angemar had been the one in possession of the rocks when captured; Zulavi had known it might be something his uneasy ally would be interested in - the symbols on the individual velvet holding-pouches alone, were hard to look at without breaking into a sweat - and then...*

"What's next, now?" Zulavi enquired, distracted as he touched the still-sore lip where the dead man's fist had struck him like a hammer of truth, enjoying another tickle of satisfaction, that this other loon had been taken care of. *Without the Knights Commander's ingenuity, they would not be standing here right now! Yes, the*

177

Tuxaman had better remember that exactly, but what was happening? Had the walnut fallen asleep or into a trance?

"Lord Tan'Xaviar?" Zulavi quested, shuffling his weight, listening but hearing nothing except Shuptah's shunted breathing. *Now what? What was the fiend up to?*

"My lord?!" Zulavi frowned at the green veil. *Still nothing. Now what indeed?*

Sweet Distraction Only Cuts so Far

Iambre woke up feeling heavy-headed and un-rested.

A quick glance at the water-clock showed the morning well-progressed into the hour of the smooth weave and usually not such a late sleeper, she was instantly annoyed with herself. It was a badly-timed lapse and with a curse to accompany the stab of nervous jitters that leapt within her core, she scrambled from bed with an urgency undoubtedly quite unbefitting a Princess.

She didn't care! Chief Eso might already be waiting with news and with that thought burning to the forefront of her mind, she paused just long enough to squat over the pot in the chamber-closet, then threw the laid-out dressing-gown over her shoulders and rushed to pull the bell-cord that would summon Ina from the servants' quarters directly adjacent to hers.

Casting her gaze around the formerly messy chamber, she suspected she'd not have long to wait. All of last night's dresses and make-up were no longer in sight, the chairs were ordered, the cushions straightened, the tea tray gone: all in all a proof of efficiency that reeked of Ina Uttorian.

She was not wrong.

Barely a handful of heartbeats later, the Patrician woman steamed into the bedchamber with a readiness to her steps that spoke of the handmaiden's willingness to face the day. As always impeccably attired - if with her usual flamboyant flair for dramatic appearances - Ina looked the picture of typical Esardan elegance today, the only concession to her Etruian affiliations being the skilful arrangement of complex braids piled atop her head.

The sight was familiar. Nothing new there, and it comforted. Still, it was with some interest that Iambre noted the handmaiden appeared to have commissioned yet another new dress. She was aware that the act of procuring new garments had turned out to be Ina's response to what the woman had collectively started calling 'the dullness of travelling', and regardless of her family-estrangement, the handmaiden could well-afford the extravaganza.

Waylaid from thoughts of Eso, Iambre hid a sly smile. No matter what might have happened in the past, Ina was still a *Patrician*, and the Patricians had never lacked for money - or so her mother had always told her with a spry hint of irony to overshadow badly-veiled envy.

She suppressed a shiver. *Well, Queen Ishjah could begrudge what she wanted.*

Iambre pulled her mind from her mother's 'issues' and smiled as Ina paused to curtsy. It may be so that Ina was many things, but even if the handmaiden had indeed sprung from one of the oldest, wealthiest families of the realm, Iambre had yet to see her break with her usual Iddian style.

On occasion, she had sometimes wondered if this was partly the reason for Ina's lack of welcome in her own birth home, and again the thought wafted to mind.

It didn't matter, of course, but plenty of other things did and though Ina's idea of 'fashionable' did perhaps not fall in vogue with Iambre's own taste, she could certainly appreciate the new Iddian-styled garment regardless. For sure, the cut was too daring for the Princess but it was flattering certainly: tightly fitted to hug Ina's hourglass curves in a floor-kissing wealth of ruffled ardass and interestingly-placed lace. She looked at the stitching and folds with a

180

critical eye but everything was immaculate, hinting of extraordinary skills that could only be associated with those tailors awarded the prestigious Golden Needle Emblem by the Guild. *Yes, this would have cost a fair ribbon or two...*

"A fair morn to you, Highness," Ina greeted, her tone muted, as she passed by Iambre with the measured steps of her usual sensuous walk. She looked relaxed, but the narrow-eyed look of assessment she meted out as she steered towards the bed and began straightening the sheets, was not. *Ina did not have to do this task, which spoke volumes.*

"And a fair morn to you as well, Mistress Uttorian," Iambre offered with a glimmer of wryness.

"So is My Lady well this morning?" Ina enquired as she began to fluff up the pillows.

"I am well enough," Iambre told her and yawned.

Ina gave her a look from the corner of her eye, but her tone remained light, "So My Lady appears wistful this morning but also better rested. Does this mean that Her Grace feels up for a full day of festivities?"

Iambre twisted into a stretch, then gave Ina a pointed look. "As ever, your thoughts flow straight to the point, but if I do appear wistful, it is simply caused by the late hour. You may rest assured that I am quite well, thank you."

Eying the woman as she shuffled around the bed in her new creation, Iambre added, "I see though that just in case I were not quite right, you have come prepared to sway my attention whilst you fuss and pretend not to send for the Medic. That *is* a new dress, I believe?"

181

"Oh so cunning you are, My Lady," Ina smiled, perfecting a contrite countenance to match insincere chagrin to be so easily called to task, "and so I stand guilty as charged indeed, though in truth, I would probably have worn the dress regardless, so really..."

"It's lovely." Iambre complimented with a critiquing eye. "Just 'you' in fact."

"Thank you, My Lady. I just had it delivered after visiting the temple yesterday. Less than a full day from commissioning to completion! I know it is but a simple cut but I'd say that your name alone is enough to turn the seamstresses' fingers twice as flighty as a herd of spooked toledo gazelles."

"Ina! Oh, but you didn't!" Iambre was crestfallen. "There was no need. We are here for over a full week."

"Ah... well, yes... that is true My Lady, but... "Ina winked with a conspirator's wicked glint in her eye.

"But what?" Iambre questioned, suspicions slowing her words.

Ina blinked innocently. "Well, I really shouldn't be telling you this, but I have been reliably informed that every tailor's with a name to trust will be packed to the ceilings with work in little over a day. So you see... I simply could not afford to wait."

"Really?"

"Uh-hum." Ina caught her eye briefly as she tucked-in the bed cover, "Oh and so I have taken the liberty of commissioning a surprise for all the rest of you too. However, the specific details are for later, My Lady. All I can reveal to alleviate your peaked curiosity is that a certain 'maid' in the service of the Master of Banquet's lady-wife, did reveal onto me that there is going to be a masked ball."

"Oh really?" Iambre drawled, partly because she was readily sick with the thought of Ina commissioning her anything to do with

182

'wardrobe', and partly because the woman was simply charmingly incorrigible. To stop herself from prying into what the handmaiden might have 'cooked up', Iambre forced a smooth change of subject, "So about your dress, Mistress Uttorian... I do so hope that you have not put the poor seamstresses under undue stress in my name! Such a thing would be of poor note for my reputation, as well you know!"

"My Lady, I would never presume..." Ina gasped, pretending to be hurt, but the glint in her hooded eyes reassured Iambre she was not at all ill-touched by her Mistress' caution - a fact that was obvious when next Ina blinked innocently under Iambre's scrutiny and teased, "However, I should probably tell My Lady that some fingers were rumoured to have almost fallen off during their heroic effort to finish my demands. Uh, and the blood and the mess-"

"Oh enough of your Esardan humour! I do not have the capacity to care about half a dozen distraught locals whilst we reside here." Iambre waved a hand whilst she kept a good-natured expression, hoping that Ina was truly just joking about the stressed seamstresses. The Esardans were well known to always be the first to pollute their humour with references to bits of gore and guts, but with the image of a dirty jackal fight riding in the back of her mind, Iambre just could not stomach the idea of blood right then. *Klaas had to have news...*

To distract herself - *she must keep her aplomb!* - Iambre tapped her lip and turned a pensive eyed onto Ina. "You inspire curiosity - and see now I am tempted to ask what price said seamstresses were able to exact for such a furious pace of work, uh, but I wonder... do I really want to find out?"

183

"Ah Highness, you are indeed clever,-" Ina intoned with a wink over one shoulder as she tugged down the final corner of the quilted bed-spread and started towards the nearest window, "-and lest you ask me outright I shall not answer for fear that it was the contents of my purse and not you name that saw the lady-proprietor so eager to please my demands. Now, what are your wishes for this morning, My Lady?"

'To borrow a little of your confidence', Iambre wanted to say but instead, she shrugged. With a certain longing for home rushing through her, she sent the handmaiden's bared shoulders and lace sleeves one last wistful glance, then forced herself onto business.

"I have an early appointment with Chief Eso," she announced, the tone light. "Has she perchance called yet?"

"My Lady, as of yet I have not seen the Chief." Ina pulled at the heavy cord to lift back the gilt curtains and let in a cool dash of sunlight that made the iridescent yellow-blues and indigo of her dress flash as she moved, "Do you wish for me to summon her?"

"My thanks to you Ina, yes if you would be so kind? I have other matters to attend shortly but I must see the Chief beforehand."

Ina nodded, "I shall see to it personally, My Lady."

As if the thought of navigating the vast lengths of Castle Zanzier's corridors was of no greater concern to her, Ina went to the next window and repeated the procedure until the bedroom lay covered in a haze of cold autumnal sun. The addition of light revealed to Iambre the dizzying pattern within patterns within the weaves of Ina's new dress and she wondered why she should still feel so surprised every time she saw this style. The Esardan people coveted these odd decorations upon everything they owned, right from the murals that so often filled entire lengths of walls within their

184

airy houses, right down to their clothes and even the rich caparisons adorning their horses - and she breezily wondered if Ina had ever owned a piece of clothing that didn't bear some sort of crazy pattern, geometric or other. Probably not - but she couldn't fault Ina for the tradition. They were far from home and-

She severed thought. Mood darkening with memories of home, she knew not why she should feel so fragile but it was a sensation she could not allow to brew. With plans scheduled for two meetings and one late luncheon, her day was nowhere near as full as it might have been but she must keep her mind on the present or the unfortunate representatives would find a quivering, homesick girl in place of a would-be Queen!

All of that was later though. First, she must concentrate on how to handle Eso; think about what she wanted to say or else the Chief of Security would run hoops around her, another thing she could not allow to happen either!

Iambre suppressed a sigh. Last night's late ponderings had brought her nowhere nearer to concocting a feasible plan in regards to how she might serve to make herself useful, and in its place, she was left with the vague hope that Eso would simply come to her with good news this morning. *Still... just in case she didn't-*

"Highness, I will be going then," Ina interrupted. She bobbed into a short curtsy and started leaving, but Iambre had a sudden inkling and called her back.

"I take it that Palea is out?" The Princess forced her face into an agreeable mask.

Ina nodded, "Why yes. Since early, My Lady. I have not seen her come back yet."

Iambre shook her head, "Oh it's fine, but could you perhaps have a care to look for her whilst you're out? If you locate her, ask her to see to some breakfast."

"My Lady." Ina obliged with a small nod and glided through the discrete door of the handmaidens' shared quarters with a swish of fabric and a ruffle of skirts; if she was surprised that Iambre did not want her help in getting dressed, she did not show.

Of course, Ina still knew nothing about the problems Iambre was joggling in her mind but she must have sensed the Princess' impatient mood, for she was not long in re-appearing, this time with a veil draped over one arm as she closed the hidden panel of the servants' door with a soft click. Then, without pausing to afford herself the aid of a mirror, she unfurled and twirled the length of fabric, artfully drawing the pale-blue chiffon over the coiled knoll of twined, interlacing plaits atop her head. Obscuring but never entirely hiding, the veil fell across the woman's features as intended, swaying stiffly before Ina confidently reached to hold it in place with one hand, using the other to secure the symbol of her status with a twist of jewelled hairpins as she glided towards the outer doors.

Smoothing the veil with her fingers so that it would hang in orderly, stiff ripples to her hips, Ina offered Iambre a small nod in passing. *Dependable Ina... Gods...*

Iambre watched her go with a nervous stab of needles to her abdomen but she knew she couldn't allow herself to linger in this state of agitation, so she resolutely went to start her ablutions. A princess she might be, but she was at least perfectly capable of seeing herself through her own morning routine when needed and it was a thing she enjoyed today, for without anyone to preen or prick, powder or dress, life seemed just a little more private; a little less demanding.

Pouring now less-than-tepid water from a white jug into the impossibly ornate swan-shaped hand basin, her mind wandered, soon orbiting familiar concerns.

Well damn Solancei, why did she always have to worry about her? Why? She wished they'd never made her friend swear those Oaths or sign those golden documents - as though... as though signing her life away was such a grand honourable thing when really it was more as though someone had hung a downward sword over her cousin's head with a piece of string, nothing but a hair's worth away from severing.

Iambre rubbed some soap into the intended cloth with vigour birthed from a garter of irritation. *Well, at least, she didn't have Ina to worry about,* she thought with a flux of sour amusement, *only perhaps the woman's eye-turning backside!*

Again, she felt a trickle of reluctant awe for the older woman. Seemed that the handmaiden had once more proven that 'looking both alluring and demure' was indeed one of her greatest tricks. Her mother would've disapproved, *of course,* just as she'd spent the last two years disapproving that Iambre should so openly flaunt her connection with this blatant Patrician 'hussy'.

Of course, Iambre had always suspected that since her mother was in fact of Valdéran roots herself, the woman had probably been under subtle pressure from that side of her family to forward one 'her own' into close service of her daughter. And really, why not?

In spite History, or maybe because of it, the last old families were well-known to promote themselves and theirs whenever possible; Ishjah's inability to influence her daughter's preference for a companion would have been 'an issue', as would the constant idea of her daughter entertaining a handmaiden of a 'rivalling' family.

Iambre smirked to herself. She had heard her mother complain a dozen times that this certainly did not constitute Valdéran 'good practise'. The Valdérans valued intrigue and status as much as the Patricians did their wealth and the Sihnarians their warfare - and as true as the sun set each night, so would the remaining three Houses continue to stay true to their roots, even after all these centuries!

Iambre - in as much as she was able - did not condone this kind of politic. *Why scheme when honesty got you further?* It was in Ishjah's words, 'a sad philosophy inherited from her father', and one abhorred by the Queen's many supporters - yet when Iambre was Queen, she intended for the old families to work as hard as the new to gain favour. *Indeed, when she was Queen...*

Iambre grimaced and shook her head to dispel the image as she rinsed and lathered and washed. *That day,* was thankfully still far away and until then, she expected her mother to continue her 'hints', just as she expected herself to continue 'the ignoring' - and wasn't that just the most perfect 'pick me up' in response to her bout of homesickness: the blessed absence of her mother; the thought of tangled, old politicians...

So let her mother's Valdéran roots hang! Ina was so much more loyal to her home-city of Iddia than she'd ever been to her Patrician family and that was enough. Yes, Lancei and Ina might have the occasional spat of icy disagreements but it was a manageable 'hazard'. Ina's knowledge of the world was astounding, and her often racy stories served to fill the boring days of travelling much better than any book of fables or myths. Even Palea thought so - though she pretended to be scandalised.

Valdéran or no - surely her own mother could see the benefit of having one of the Patricians' own to advise her daughter now that they were soon to reside in the shadows of this family for a goodly while after-

Iambre threw the washcloth down with a defiant frown. *No, she would not go there! Would not finish that thought, because it meant thinking about a time when Bilan was no longer supposed to be relevant; where he no longer shared a part in her life.*

Finishing up at the washstand and wiggling the reminder of the way out of her nightdress, Iambre padded across the bed chamber wearing nothing but goosebumps to look at the coffers in her dressing room. Sniffing and wiping her eyes with brash swipes that left her momentarily sightless, a deep breath forced her mind to centre on the now. Some of her older gowns had not yet been unpacked but after a short rummage, she managed to pull forth appropriate smalls and a plain floor-length dress complete with blue over-skirts.

Styled to lace-up at the sides, it took relatively little effort to dress and she soon pulled the last loop of midnight-blue lacings into a secure bow with a feeling of contentment riding softly on the back of her mundane achievement. *Such a small thing, and yet...*

On the spur of casting a glance in the mirror, she decided - for the sake of appearances - to also don the silver belt of slim interlocking hoops that Commander Zulavi had offered her as 'a token of his esteem' upon the night of their arrival. She didn't actually wish to be seen bearing anything the vile man had bestowed but neither did she wish to appear discourteous and for no other reason, than it would make her seem the better person, Iambre hooked the section of metal around her waist, letting the spare length fall to mid-calf

189

amidst the heavy skirts. *There! Thankfully, it was barely visible. Now let's see though, what manner of reception this would bring her!*

A Meeting with the Tuxaman Loon

"Patrician? My Lord, are you there?" Zulavi questioned, a hint of impatience welling up. *Still nothing. What was this then?*

The silence pulled at him. The loon was-

"So will you join me?" echoed the Patrician's voice with a tinge of exasperation from 'the somewhere' beyond the light.

Inexplicably jolted, Zulavi rushed, "Yes. Yes of course. Why were you not responding? What happened?"

Tan'Xaviar hissed, "Minor adjustment was needed. You needn't worry."

Zulavi felt exasperation roll through his body but pushed for the heat to drain.

"I await your instruction. How do we do this?" he demanded, the impatience spilling out as the lingering memory of Angemar brought his gaze to the chamber's simple water clock in memory of other tasks in need of his attention before this evening.

It was still just mid-morning but the clock's single hand was jumping without fault towards the hour of the smooth weave. If he did not get done with the day's tasks he would not have time to check in on *that woman* after all, and Gods be good but the idea of that encounter had his sense of anticipation twitching far more readily than the idea of this imminent face-to-face with the Tuxaman nut.

"How?" he repeated when once again, an answer did not seem to be instantly forthcoming. Eying the symbols and the stones at his feet, he was reminded of how specific both the Patrician Lord, and eventually Angemar Cillario, had been in their instructions on the size of the circle as well as the positioning of the stones in relation to said-symbols. Too small and the circle would apparently oppress the ability of the stones to function in relation to their appointed 'cyphers'; too large and the circle would not spring the power as directed due to loss of 'focus'. *Apparently, to activate the stones, one must apply accuracy to one's endeavour; a thing that had seemed as ludicrous as the idea of using blood, and yet now it flecking worked!*

Zulavi glanced at the narrow strip of linen that bandaged his cut palm. *Any more like this and he'd look as though he'd been in a melee! Blood was needed. One's own to be exact.* It had remained a fact that even Visentor Tan'Xaviar had known nothing about. As much as he'd tried, the loon had been unable to find any supporting information in any of his numerous scrolls, whilst Angemar - *curse his admirable resistance* - had known all along, yet had also happily failed to 'volunteer' for quite a goodly while. *And that had cost them. A whole damnable season of late or lost messages - but no more now! No more!*

"Now my good liege, please recall what I told you...-" Visentor's voice strained, then crackled a little and fizzled below hearing a few heartbeats. To Simarovien Zulavi it sounded as though the Patrician was further away than before then, or as though he'd been speaking through some kind of odd interference, but then the sound cleared, "-...it will be my pleasure to unveil just what the Vidaria Stones can do."

Zulavi hesitated just a beat; the 'my liege' title was pleasing but it didn't fool him. *This could be a trick or a genuine show of the stones' abilities; did he truly trust?*

"Lord Commander, I may be half a realm away," Visentor's hollow voice echoed, a little vexed, "but I sense your hesitation just the same. You will have to trust in my knowledge as well as in our agreement! Let me remind you now that I am the one who stands to lose so much more than you could ever dream if our plans were to go the slightest bit awry, so do not question my sincerity when I guarantee you this is perfectly safe."

Sighing at his Aide, Simarovien shrugged his shoulders as though to casually to prepare himself. Visentor's words made sense but by the look of Shuptah's face, he might as well be contemplating a walk through a wall of burning acid, but at least the man's obvious disbelief made Simarovien smile. *Shuptah was far too busy worrying for the both of them to even recognize similar doubts in his Master's mind. Which was good...*

Determined to dawdle no longer, Simarovien took two rapid strides forward-

"Be mindful of your pace, Commander!"

The loon's sharp warning jolted Simarovien to a stop mid-stride, just as his foot lifted to cross the perimeter threshold and the Knights Commander issued a vexed hiss of alarm as he rapidly shifted away from the light.

Oblivious, Visentor said, "Only, beware Commander. Recall that if you disturb the circle or the stones at any time, at the very least it might break our connection; at the very worst, however, we could perhaps trigger a calamity! I would beg you not to... not to be careless!"

"Gods' pestilence man!" Zulavi exploded, then drew a deep breath to calm the useless flow of sudden anger. In a tone of light sarcasm, he said, "Tan'Xaviar, think you might have mentioned that small matter *before* suggesting that I step into this... *thing!?* Now are there any other 'incidental' insights you need to recount before I do this or am I safe to proceed?"

On a sudden whim - aware that he'd already given the Patrician too many advantages today - Simarovien Zulavi did not wait for the man to answer before he simply threw caution to the wind and stepped forward. Of course he took a care not to disturb a thing, and by the intake of breath behind him, he guessed that Shuptah must be preparing to greet Osari'Chi himself at the sight of his Master's bold audacity. Then Simarovien lost all further interest in the aide or what he might do or say when for a split heartbeat, the air seemed to cool alarmingly all around him.

He felt it - more than he saw it - when he actually breached the unseen border held within that green wave of light then. It was not unpleasant. It was not even surprising. Somehow it felt quite natural, as though he'd already done this countless times: the ensuing feeling of displacement was brief, and-

Zulavi blinked, then found himself as promised within the circle's sanctum. *Alone.*

That should have disturbed him - he'd expected to see Tan'Xaviar already there, but in the quiet within, Simarovien could sense no pressure of danger against his heightened senses, nor did he feel unnerved like he had done upon viewing it from the outside and he relaxed a little then. It felt to him as if the veil of brackish light surrounded him like a cocoon. Everything beyond was as it should be and except for the visual distortion, everything was easily recognisable to the naked eye. *Right from the heavy drapes with their cloth-of-gold lining now drawn tightly across each of the tall windows to blot out his and Shuptah's activities to the outside world - to the illegally-obtained pelt of a silver-leopard, still spread*

194

appealingly wide across the covers of his stout, mahogany four-poster bed: it was all so very... normal.

As though he saw it for the first time, he eyed the fine feline fur a blink longer. *It seemed fitting.* Every time he looked at the heraldic symbol of the Ostravahn Royal House sprawled across his bed, snarling mouth and all, he experienced a small stab of peace. *The skinned creature was a befitting image of the way the Crown would be heading and for a moment he considered the idea of moving the treasure onto the floor. He liked the symbolism of that too - and evenings could be cold...*

Zulavi smiled and ran his eyes randomly across the rest of the chamber: the display of weaponry across the walls, the low furniture and cloak stand, his petrified aide, the obscene maze-carved, stupidly-expensive obsidian-cloaked fireplace currently void of light, but already primed for this evening with logs of pine- and black-wood...

Yes, he thought with a small smile: everything looked in order. *Hazy order. But in order, nonetheless.*

As by way of habit, Simarovien glanced briefly towards his the outer chamber, often used as an office rather than a dressing room as intended. The door was open and he could see a sliver of the plain but well-fashioned oak door adjacent: the one that marked the entrance directly from his inner sanctum - by way of spiralling stairs - into the bowels of the castle, where the seemingly-endless passages of the old subterranean levels made up almost as big a percentage of corridors and chambers as those of the castle above. That door remained shut, of course, locked by a single large iron key, which by way of design also functioned as door handle. *One*

195

way in. One way out. Just as it had ever been. Soon he would visit the Veranto twirl. Soon...

Pushing the image of her grey gaze from mind, on a sudden whim he tilted his head back to examine the ceiling within this space. It left him near-instantly with slightly dizzying impression of the familiar white-washed surface as it danced with the eerie effect of water rippling across a narrow pool - and as the sudden onslaught of nausea gripped him, he quickly looked away before it could wreak its damage on him. *This was all very interesting but where was Tan'Xaviar?*

Tinkering as usual, offered an inspired voice in his head. *Tinkering and recording every minuscule detail, just as usual...*

Preparing to wait once more, he crossed his arms and took pleasure in his own dwindling awe. *It was hardly surprising.* Out there on his 'Western-perch', in the furthermost reaches of the realm, Visentor Tan'Xaviar's home province was obviously considered a little 'backward' by most of the more 'sophisticated' provinces - however, for a man of Tan'Xaviar's roots and tastes, it probably neared perfection. In result, as it were, the walnut was probably busy documenting every small act of this event in one of those leather-bound, sweet-smelling collection-books of his. Very bookish - *and very annoying, yes* - but Simarovien had not chosen the man as his ally on the basis of his sane conduct or likeable spirits. If you pushed the man, he became obstinate, but there were other ways to handle the young loon.

Zulavi shifted, rubbing his chin pensively as he considered his fellow noble. Tan'Xaviar loved flattery. It was as though the man breathed it in when offered. He also loved to lecture: the Patrician noble should have been a scholar, Simarovien mused, except...

Visentor held only twenty-six summers to his life, but little-known knowledge - bought and paid for with various favours or monies or both - had assured Zulavi that the aristocrat had lost his 'rocks' several years ago - and not in a respectable, eccentric way like some, either. No, the man had some creepy habits - *'hobbies' really* - and it was something Simarovien had unfortunately managed to confirm first hand too!

He twisted from the unsavoury memories collected during his most recent visit.

The Tuxaman was a hermit so perhaps it made sense that he pursued and obtained these oddities whilst a skeleton crew maintained his mansion by the lake, but the palace was a beautiful as an abandoned mausoleum. Add to that the question of Tan'Xaviar's 'inheritance' and his lacking willingness to step up and seize the mantle of responsibilities, and then...

Zulavi knew it had spelt disaster for the entire realm - if the man did not possess an agreeable nature in private, he'd be even less desirable for anything of official nature - however, due to their tidy arrangement, the realm would not suffer the effects of this Patrician imbecile after all. Luckily, the loon was bewitched by his own quest for knowledge. Rumours, inbreeding, and other nauseating stories aside: how else would anyone go willingly into those old Tuxaman catacombs in order to dig through ossuaries and crumbling cave-ins in search of latent mysteries or shrouded treasures and scripts? How else could anyone enjoy those... *those other things the loon seemed so perversely fond of?*

He killed a mild shiver. If he didn't stop to think too hard on the matter, he could of course live with his 'discoveries' - however, truthfully, seeing the man at work was whole other matter! The

Knights Commander was not beyond certain crooked pleasures if it served his purposes, but witnessing Tan'Xaviar halfway through the process of vivisecting a woman, whilst attending documents and muttering what sounded suspiciously like incantations...

Zulavi could see the man in his mind's eye: meticulously carving strips of skin from her medicated body; carefully recording every detail - taking his terrible, sweet time to document how his ministrations slowly turned the victim into a dried, living cadaver...

An experiment. That was how the Patrician had described his undertakings, grinning with a strange hint of excitement as they'd sat down for dinner later that day. *The Patrician had been at it for weeks. Keeping that woman alive: changing her. No torture for knowledge or to settle slights or other ill-begotten deeds, no - just an experiment...*

Zulavi swallowed. *That stench of putrefied flesh had been revolting; had stayed with him for long after leaving Tuxama Lake. He'd rather disembowel a man any day and watch him die!* Sure, Tan'Xaviar had not gone as far as showing him 'the collection' but Zulavi had heard of it and now knew it must exist.

Maybe when his own plans were progressed, he could do away with the Patrician, he speculated, because from that kind of amusements there could be no saving short of a permanent relocation to the cellars of a far-away asylum, of course.

Squashing the uneasy pleasure of such thought, Zulavi still had to admit that whether a loon or not, he did not trust the Patrician not to negate upon their agreement. After all, who'd willingly give away the kind of power Visentor Tan'Xaviar stood but a stone's throw from inheriting? Zulavi shifted his weight, eyes never quite resting.

What was taking the nut so long? Was this a trick after all? Had he missed something?

"Greetings anew My Lord Commander!" Visentor's unexpectedly clear voice jumped Simarovien abruptly from his reflections once more. In utter failure to appear aloof, he took a step back in consternation before he could think to halt his own reaction - then he simply stared when the hollow voice of his Tuxaman accomplice suddenly gained a face and body as the man appeared inexplicably - and quite simply - out of thin air.

"So... have your eyes had their fill yet?" his queer ally droned on, "Or do you require another moment to adjust? I can wait a little. Oh, I'll grant you that the view within this bubble, is hardly the thing that would impress a hardened sceptic like yourself; certainly, it does not impress me much either, but *seeing* you here, however..."

Lord Tan'Xaviar's stocky form had not altered since the last time Simarovien had met him in the flesh and yet it was nothing if not disconcerting to find the man himself - solid skin and bones - right here in front of him! As always the man's broad features made the Knights Commander wonder if the Tuxaman might not have had a Kheltian ancestor or two but that was nought by idle speculation. Today, the man wore a pair of those traditional Tuxaman trousers that always seemed to be made up of a surplus of fabric - this time red and tucked into a neat pair of calf-length, pointy-toed black boots that made the loon's feet look far longer than they could possibly be.

Still, it seemed auspicious that Visentor's sleeve-less tunic was as unadorned as a commoner's today, and if the man's tawny hair was lank from neglect and his prominent cheekbones a little sharp under the otherwise lightly-tanned, stretched skin, the violet-blue eyes

199

staring directly into his, held lucid intelligence and more than a little of the usually suppressed, but ever-keen, edge of appeal for validation.

"Lord Tan'Xaviar." Simarovien stated, his greeting tepid though he chose to believe the other man's polished appearances a good sign that on this occasion he might be speaking to 'the lord' rather than 'the prophetic loon'.

Freaks and bookish scholars, his mind taunted. *Just tolerate the man but never trust him. That is one for yourself to recall!*

With the force of practical willpower, the Knights Commander strangled the odd need to ensure that the other lord was really physically present and stopped himself short before he could give in to temptation and prod the man.

However, it was as though Visentor Tan'Xaviar could read the Commander's mind for his countenance morphed with sly understanding to produce a smirk of pleasure. In a light, casual voice he said, "Yes My Lord, you might touch me if you so wish, but trust me: we are indeed both present here. In the flesh. Right now, within this circle. Wondrous, no?"

Simarovien grimaced to decline the offer as he eyed Visentor with a burst of lingering scepticism, but the man looked guileless and for a moment Simarovien waged a silent debate within whether he could have forced himself to reach for the Patrician after all. *He thought probably not...*

Visentor shrugged as though it was all the same to him, offering his ally another knowing smirk that might have meandered towards droll amusement - though right this instant, the side of the man that was ever the 'avid preacher' now returned to nil the expression in time to prevent affront.

"This is the purpose of the Vidaria Stones, then?" Zulavi questioned, looking around with a slightly skewered expression, "I imagined there'd be more."

"Hmmm…" The loon smacked his lips as though savouring an extra palatable taste left behind in his mouth. Zulavi stayed quiet and Tan'Xaviar relented with a soft sigh.

"Very well, My Lord: I would tell you that I am not certain, of course, but I seek to test a few ideas whilst we are present." He grinned. "Still, whether the documents will prove right or not, all of this should be impossible, shouldn't it? Still, you see that it's not! My Sovereign-general is surely impressed that this is extraordinary enough to begin with, no?"

Solancei's Memoirs
The Province of Tarléon.
Hilt's pass; westbound.
Autumn of 780 P. C. W.

I swear I sometimes I still hear the driver cuss aloud, but not always. Sometimes I smell the creeping evening frost on the road; sometimes I taste the fetor in the wind; sometimes I see the snatched, rapid event of a guard ripped from his mount like a rag-doll without substance, I hear severed screams or growls of the unreal; sometimes... sometimes other things are almost seen, but then not...

And sometimes...

Sometimes, I feel the fear; the false memory enough to send me weak as I seek only to hide from the world; from the future - yet other times I'm above it; and others still, I feel the drop, feel the heart leave my chest as I become momentarily weightless and see their faces, contorting as we fall...

Inside the cabin, the springs of the seat absorbed the rebound of the vehicle's erratic movement with an unnatural screech of their own. A stench reached my nostrils: little more than a tiny riff on the air, but revolting. The carriage bounced and clanged down hard. *It felt wrong too... there was a crack...*

Now breathless from worry, I steadied myself, bracing one hand against the upholstery on either side of my thighs to minimise the effects on my body. I still wanted to reach for Taliana and bury my head in her shoulder, the maddening, geometric designs of her old shawl somehow comforting, but instead I was jostled around any which way the driver swerved. A heavy force ricocheted off the side of the carriage, the bump of the impact heavy and accompanied by an angry scream that ended in a growl as the rear-wheels hit an obstacle that made the entire world skip and jump as we continued, nearly overturning.

By now the stuffy atmosphere was drenched with terror and sweat, the fresh cool notion of winter ever-present barely imaginable as we hid like burrowing rodents from the danger without. *Something polluted us all more and more. Something that crawled inside me now, like... like sentient fear!*

The vehicle swerved. Again, I was jostled abruptly along with everyone one else -Taliana exclaiming a sound of muted displeasure just as I bumped my head against the upholstered wooden panel framing the decorative row of now-veiled stained glass on my left. Sometimes, in the hag-ridden dreams that followed, this would hurt, other times it didn't; ever the first to nag and worry, my mother never seemed to notice though.

If at all possible, it deepened my concern. The adults' already pale faces had lost all colour: the low lantern light ever-portraying them as waxy corpses frozen somewhere between rigour and fleeting life.

From without, the driver shouted. The words were stolen by the wind and the isolation provided by the cabin, but I felt the carriage surge forward as his team responded, egged on by the same fear as ours, barely needing the driving whip to produce more speed. For moments longer though, the whip continued to crack too loudly over the dismembered rumble of wheels and hooves; those animals gave their all, but-

But we would not get away. Somehow the stench was worsening, bleeding into me... drenching... shouts of men echoed, then turning isolated: like harsh stolen screams, snatched away by wind and speed... a horse whinnied too... gone...

Heart lurching with understanding I shouldn't possess, I struggled to breathe. My next action seemed irrational, but suddenly I was fighting my father's retainer to reach the door-pull. I could not see those who pursued us, but I knew they wanted me: I could feel it; I had felt it all along!

As a result, a 'need' hung in the air, telling; disturbing... *a dozen people were going to die because of me! A dozen people!*

"My Lady, don't!" My father's valet yelled in horror, over and over, as he fought back against my sudden, manic onslaught - foiling my attempts to reach the door latch, even as the feral sounds and the stench of death rode ever-closer, "My Lady, don't! They will kill you!"

'And all of you too', I wanted to screech in despair, but the words ever-stuck because even if I would've been permitted to speak then, the air was rife with the stench of carrion now.

A true, feral growl sundered the atmosphere: an ancient malice drawing low like a second skin over mine. Old hatred; new hunger! Too close!

The carriage wobbled grossly as something heavy hit the roof like the dead-weight of ten oxen. The ensuing fetor floored me, even as the carriage roof seemed to rip in half and disappear. My mother screamed. It had the pitch of an injured deer in such pain, I could not relate till years later.

A snarl of hatred and violence rend the air just as shadow blackened out the emerging stars. It was the sound of death hunting; the sound of futures lost; the carriage driver yelled twice, incoherent with fear as for a heartbeat we were floating, the coach weightless, horses screaming. They sounded like my mother; everything was overturned...

Then shadow and fetor lifted and we plummeted. My mother was no longer in the carriage, but as I looked up her severed torso slammed back into the cabin compartment through the broken roof and Taliana screamed then: rage and defiance...

It was the first and only time I ever heard such heartache come out of her. I was disconnected with my own body... *we were falling...* but as I looked up at the white stars just before our broken vehicle crashed into the snow-covered ravine with devastating consequences, I saw the black-winged shadow that hovered like an unfurled sail above us.

It was not of this world.

Solancei

The story will continue in Episode 5: Notions of Risk

Available from 1st August 2018

L. L. Thomsen, *"Thank you so much for reading. As always, your reviews are greatly appreciated."*

For glossaries, maps, and more, visit the author's official website on www.llthomsen.com

Or contact via

llthomsen@themissingshield.com

www.twitter.com/LLThomsen1

www.facebook.com/linda.thomsen.12979

www.facebook.com/themissingshield/

www.instagram.com/llthomsen/?hl=en